James's Baby Girls

A romantic DDLG and ABDL love story about a Daddy who trains not one but two baby girls in the DDLG kink

By Tina Moore

Table of Contents

Chapter 1

I was the typical track queen in college. I had long blonde hair, big blue eyes, and a smile that never let me down. I was the type of girl who silenced a crowd as I walked past and who was never in short supply of boys who wanted to date me. For those four years at college, my life had been in no uncertain terms, blessed.

Yet, I wasn't at college anymore, and those days of boys waiting in line to date me were long over. The carefree days of college were long behind me as she sat in my office cubicle and looked miserably at the clock on the wall.

At this point, I knew I was dreaming. I didn't work in an office. I worked in a hospital. That was the good thing about lucid dreaming. I could watch myself have an alternative lifestyle but still be able to know what was real and what was just dreaming. I rolled over and smiled as I fell back into the dream.

I had graduated college shortly after an ankle injury and knew how lucky I was to have been given the job I now hated. After having spent four years barely passing my subjects in favor of perfecting my athletic abilities, I was not particularly qualified. Sure, I had my piece of paper saying I had graduated with an arts degree, but I never thought I would actually have to use the degree. But as the doctors confirmed my worst fears, that my running career and Olympic dreams were now out of reach, I had quickly found a job selling life insurance at a big company in the city.

"I need these on my desk by Friday," my boss said as he walked past. He hadn't even bothered to look at me, he never did. I was a long shot from the girl I used to be. No longer did I have an athletic body, I had gained over 20pounds in the five years I had been working at the job. No longer did I have my beautiful long blonde hair and had opted for a short brown bob. I often would look in the mirror and not even recognize the woman staring back at me.

"Sure thing Mr Tims," I replied, trying to smile.

I can't keep feeling this way. I thought to myself as I searched online for a gym.

This might be ok for some women. I honestly don't care how they feel about their bodies. This isn't ok for me. This isn't who I am, I am Sophie Marks, I am beautiful, and right now, I couldn't feel less beautiful within myself, I thought booking myself into the afternoon consult.

I didn't think about anything else for the next four hours of my shift. In fact, I was surprised that I didn't think of getting back into shape or even staying in shape sooner.

Maybe I was punishing myself for not going to the Olympics or something, I thought, watching the clock. It was 4:30, and I knew that come 5 o'clock, I would be out of there. No working later tonight, no going to the frozen yogurt store after work today and definitely no medium chips at 7:30 when I was bored with what was on TV. I was determined to get my health back on track.

Five o'clock finally came around, and I lept out of my chair, shut down my computer, and walked out of the office with a confidence I had not felt for years.

Walking down the street, I couldn't help the smile on her face as I walked past people who seemed to get out of my way. Usually, people would frown at me for the space I took, but today felt different. It was as though they knew I was not a person to be messed with, and if I was honest with myself, I had missed that feeling.

I turned the corner and saw the big blue building. I sighed, suddenly feeling overwhelmed by the task I had set for myself. It would be no small feat designing the body I wanted, and I knew that it was going to be hard work.

"Hi, I'm Kelly. I have an appointment with Cleo," I said to the girl behind the desk.

"Hey, um actually, Cleo called in sick about thirty minutes ago. Would you be happy with another trainer, or did you really want her?" The friendly woman behind the counter said.

"Another trainer is fine," I said with a smile. The woman behind the counter typed on her keyboard before looking back up.

"Right, so I've booked you in with Alex. He is really lovely, and here he is. Perfect timing," she said, causing me to turn around.

"Hi," Alex said, reaching out his hand and shaking mine warmly. I smiled at him.

"Let's get this paperwork filled out, and we can talk about what your goals are and such. What do you say?" He asked. I nodded my head and followed him into the office. I sat down, and he gave me a vitamin water and protein ball while I filled out the paperwork and the signing up forms.

"How committed are you to these goals? They are pretty significant," Alex asked, looking at me.

"These last five years have been really tough, and I've really let myself go. I don't want to feel this way anymore. I got a full ride through college because my track performance. I was on target to going to the Olympics, but then I hurt my ankle, and I think I've been punishing myself ever since. Look, this is the girl I really am," I said, taking out my phone and showing Alex the photos of the girl I used to be. He was clearly shocked by the look on his face, and I just gave a half-smile when he looked back at me.

"I'll help you get that girl back. Hell, maybe we even make a new girl because you can't really go backward," he said reaching out to take my hand.

"Can we start tomorrow?" I asked softly. Alex looked at me, the way his eyes sparkled made me feel both nervous and excited.

"Yeah, I think that would be a good idea. Then you can be my project, and I will do anything I want with you," he said, his face going from soft and gentle to angry and dominating as he began disappearing as I fully woke up to a deafening noise in the neighboring apartment.

It was just a dream. He isn't here, and he can't hurt you now, I said to myself. Alex, the man I had worked so hard to forget, still managed to weasel his way into my dreams. I was grateful for the noise. I didn't know what it was or who was doing it. All I knew was, every day, at 7 am, the noise started. Luckily, I had to wake up early most days. It served as an alarm clock, and honestly, it didn't bother me much anymore. I blinked my eyes open, looked at the ceiling and sighed before kicking off the covers. I was a morning person. But today seemed like the kind of day where I could have easily stayed in bed for hours. It was that lonely feeling of waking up all alone, cuddling your pillow at night when you needed extra warmth, and sometimes crying when you needed attention. I mean, I had a lot of friends at the hospital where I worked and even out of it. I made friends with everyone, the other nurses, the doctors, and even some of the patients. I had always just been super friendly like that. But sometimes, the feeling that came with friendship just wasn't enough. I needed something more, and all these acquaintances just weren't cutting it.

I arrived at work just as my shift started and after signing in, headed to get changed. As I was tieing my shoes, my best friend, Thea, walked in and sat down next to me. I was always excited to see her. There was just something about her presence, that made me feel happy. I started bouncing on the balls of my feet.

"Thea," I said, rushing to hug her. With how busy we were, it was surprising to see her at work, so I had to take my chances where I got them. She hugged me and pulled me into her arms. See, this is what I meant. My friends were very affectionate. We loved hugging each other, kissing each other and telling each other, "I love you." But it lacked that thing which only a romantic relationship could bring. It lacked intimacy.

As I melted into her embrace, another nurse came in and kissing me on my cheek, Thea broke our embrace.

"Okay, babes, see you later," I said as I stood and began to walk out of the room.

"Don't forget about tomorrow!" she

exclaimed. I frowned, but I was already out of the changing room and standing in the busy corridor. I didn't want to turn back to ask her what was going to happen the next day. It was going to be Saturday. Nothing exciting ever happened on Saturdays. Except maybe she slept over or something. And since she had a boyfriend, that had become extremely rare. I shook my head and walked away. I figured she was going to tell me after our shift. We always messaged after work. She would tell me the funny or sad things that happened in her day, and I would do the same. She called me her work-wife as I was the only person would she had told all her deepest secrets and fears to. I liked that she felt she could trust me, and over many a bottle of wine, we had watched our friendship grow.

***

The day was a long one, and as I was changing back into my casual clothes, all I wanted to do was go home and sleep. But Thea had other ideas. Apparently, she was coming home with me tonight. She had sent me a message during my shift, asking for me to wait with her by the parking lot. It was in this text she had told me that she was coming home with me.

"Don't tell me you forgot about it?" she asked as soon as she joined me at the parking lot of the hospital. I frowned.

"Forget about what? Can you stop speaking in riddles?" I asked, rolling my eyes. Couldn't she just say it? And stop telling me I had forgotten. I knew I had forgotten. If I hadn't, she wouldn't have been telling me.

"The function, stupid! The function! It's the first one that we were invited to, and you forget?" I widened my eyes. The fact that the function was tomorrow had completely escaped my mind.

"You know I've had a lot on my mind," I said, and she nodded sadly. She wasn't my best friend for nothing. We knew basically everything there was to know about each other.

"It's okay, babes. You'll be fine," Thea said, and I sighed. I didn't respond to that with anything, just walked to my car, and got in.

I turned the radio on loudly so that Thea didn't try to say anything more, and I am glad she took the hint. She was good like that, and I was grateful to have a friend who actually understood me. I also think Thea had realized that her answer had been a little insensitive, especially for someone who had a significant other. I honestly didn't begrudge her, I just hated those *you'll be fine,* and *everything will be okay* answers. After going through a drive-through and getting something to eat, Thea and I reached home. I hated that I was a comfort eater and had ordered two big burgers and a chocolate shake. Tomorrow was going to be a big day. I could feel it.

***

I was not wrong about the day being a big one! Thea and I had gone shopping for the outfits we were going to wear to the function. True to form, Thea had gone for a little black number that hugged all her beautiful curves. It had thin straps at the back and showed off her toned back muscles. She was so beautiful; it was not surprising she never had trouble finding a boyfriend. I had been shopping for three hours by the time I found my dress. I was about to give up and settle for something I already owned when I saw a scarlet red piece of fabric poking out at the back of the store. I walked over and took it down from the hanger. It was stunning, with a low cut V-neckline that I knew would show off my cleavage. I tried it on and looked at myself in the mirror and ran my hands over my curves. It made me feel sexy. It made me feel like a woman, and I knew that a lot of eyes were going to be on me in this dress.

Thea and I took our sweet time getting ready. I wanted to look good. I wanted attention tonight, and I was determined to get it. I showered first, letting the water wash away any insecurity that reared its ugly head. I cleaned, shaved, perfumed, and moisturized my body before leaving the bathroom with just my pink towel wrapped loosely around my toned body. I walked into my bedroom and winked at Thea as she passed me and headed into the bathroom to shower. I waited until I heard the shower water running before I dropped my towel and walked into the kitchen to pour myself a drink. Even if it was just soda, the action of opening a bottle and pouring the contents into a glass was therapeutic. I took a sip and smiled.

Tonight was going to be good. Walking back into my room, I went to my lingerie drawer and ran my hands over the lace material. I selected the panties and a bra in the same color as my dress and smiled as I put it on. I had managed to keep some tan from the summer, and the color made me feel as though I was in Spain all over again. I pulled on my dress just as Thea got out of the shower, and she instinctively came behind me and zipped up the back zipper. Soon enough, she was also ready, and we touched up each other's makeup before kissing the mirror on the way out of the house. We always did this, and the mirror by my front door was covered in different shades of lipstick. Just as I grabbed the front door handle, Thea placed her hand over mine and paused before she repeated what she always did on nights like this one. I sighed and rolled my eyes, knowing what was coming next. I had heard her speech so many times. I could repeat it by heart.

"No drinks from strangers, no rides from strangers..." she started, and I finished "and no kisses from strangers." Maybe it sounded weird, but to us, it wasn't. Thea knew how crazy I could get, especially under the influence of alcohol, even if it was just one glass. I had always been that way, and she had rescued me from myself and the precarious situations I had almost put myself in more times than I could count. That was why I stayed away from alcohol, especially at work functions like the one we were about to be attending. Alcohol and I well, we hated each other.

"We'll have fun, babe," Thea reassured me then placed a kiss on my forehead.

***

We had arrived about ten minutes late, but it wasn't an issue because events like this were always just a loosely timed affair. We entered the function, and I was surprised by how elegantly the venue had been decorated. I liked the music which was playing, and I loved seeing how everyone looked out of scrubs. I had stopped to say hi to everyone I knew then I headed to the bar. I knew the bartender would be shocked when I ordered a plain soda most people usually were, and as my prediction was correct, he looked at me curiously before passing me my drink. I sighed with a feeling somewhere between frustration and loneliness, and walked to a corner of the room and sipped on my drink in the shadows. I was usually more bubbly than this, but all the pointless, empty small talk had taken my spirit away. I was in no mood to do the things I often enjoyed. So I settled for the next best thing. I was watching people doing what I usually enjoyed.

I was watching people when I spotted him. Our eyes met for a while, then someone called for his attention. I sighed a little and let my eyes linger elsewhere, all the while sipping on my soda. Then I started wondering what kind of lives the people in the room lived behind their closed doors. I always enjoyed thinking what kind of dirty things people got up behind their suburban lifestyles. With their tennis on the weekend and country club membership, these were always the most sexually depraved people. Watching them and making up stories about all the filthy things they got up to always brought a smile to my face. For example, the guy with the adorable glasses on his head. He was a lonely doctor, and this was the only time he had to go out. So he took this opportunity thinking it would be nice to socialize with people instead of having a another night jerking off alone to an online anime dating site. I wasn't even sure anime dating sites existed, but I figured there'd be something like this on the internet, it was the interest after all.

"Not feeling tonight, are we?" I turned to look at who had rudely interrupted my thought process and saw that it was the man whose eyes I had met when he was on the dance floor. He was even more attractive up close. Then I realized he had asked me a question. I smiled a little sardonically.

"Not really I guess," I replied looking up at him

"This is not your scene?" he asked, and I smiled a little. If only he knew.

"It is. I'm just out of it tonight, I guess," I explained, looking up to meet his beautiful grey eyes.

"Oh. It's one of those nights," he said, and I nodded absently, taking another sip out of my soda. This was weird. Usually, I always had something to say to people. Especially when they were young and hot like the man who was standing next to me. Besides, hadn't I been crying the whole morning about how lonely I was? Why didn't I just take the reins of the conversation and see if the mister was open for dialogue? As I was about to say something, he beat me to it and said, "I'm James. You?"

"I'm Kelly," I said shyly, taking the hand that he had extended. What was happening to me?!

"Beautiful name," James said, smiling. His smile was maybe one of the most beautiful things I had ever seen in my life. It was so beautiful. Fuck.

"Thank you. I'm a nurse at Weiss Memorial. I assume you're a doctor?" I asked, regaining my tempo a little. His serious and grave air just screamed doctor. I could be wrong, though.

"Yes, I am actually. I usually don't attend these... things," James said. Aha. I was right. I couldn't help but laugh at the way he said "things." It was almost like he was physically pained.

"And pray tell, what is wrong with these

things?" I asked, with a small smile at the corner of my lip. I didn't want to pass off as the weirdo who laughed at everything.

"People," he said miserably, and I couldn't help but let out a soft sound. The expression on his face looked too sad to be serious, though, so I laughed.

"And you? Can I ask why tonight is off? Or are you a closet people hater like me?" James asked, and I sighed a little. I debated with myself for some time. For a weird reason, I felt really comfortable with this man that I had just met. So I threw caution to the wind and said, "I'm lonely. And I'm tired of being lonely."

"You don't have any friends?" he asked, and I rolled my eyes.

"That's not what I meant. I mean, I'm tired of searching for a physical and emotional connection with someone. It's exhausting," I mumbled the last part, a little reluctant to look at him now. I had just shared my deepest wishes with a total stranger. He probably thought I was really weird.

"And what if I told you you had found them?" James asked, and I looked up at him sharply. He smiled.

"Let's do this. You give me your number, and we fix up something later on. What do you say?" James asked, smiling like someone who already knew all my secrets.

"Yes," I said timidly, a bit out of character because I was shocked. I definitely hadn't been expecting something like that. I put my number in his phone, and after placing a chaste kiss on my forehead, he walked away with a promise to call me.

"Who was that *hottie*?" Thea asked as she slinked up next to me silently. I was already used to her doing that, so I wasn't startled.

"Guess who just got her number taken by a hot dude?" I fangirled hard, smiling broadly at Thea. She squealed then hugged me

"Fingers crossed bitch," she said.

"Fingers crossed," I reiterated.

***

James and I had certainly made something happen and three months since James and I had been seeing each other. After the night at the function, we were inseparable. We were practically glued to each other on weekends since both of us had full schedules during the week. It was awesome and exciting, and everything that I had spent all that time searching for and I knew that tonight was going to be just as amazing all of the previous evenings together. I knew that I was finally ready for us to take it to the next step. He was coming over for dinner like he did almost every Saturday. But what he didn't know was that this time around, I was dessert. It was the first time that we were going to have sex. I just hadn't been ready before. But tonight, I had planned a whole surprise for him. I just hoped he didn't react negatively.

I was wearing a long t-shirt when he came in. I

didn't want to dress up in anything fancy because I wanted it to be a complete surprise. So I had stayed on the simple side. Dinner had gone well like it always did, with loads of banter and laughter. He made me smile. I just couldn't help it when I was around him.

"Time for dessert," I said, smiling as I came to take his dishes away from the table.

"Babe. I'm stuffed," he said, and I just smiled.

"Trust me. You'll like it," I reassured him, making sure to be a bit cryptic. I went to the kitchen, took off my t-shirt, then lay on the counter.

"Babe," I called out.

"Come to the kitchen," I added. I heard James's footsteps approaching, and I heard his gasp when he saw me lying there with my legs spread wide. I was wearing a matching light pink linger set with my blonde waves tumbling down over my shoulders and nipples.

"Kelly," James started when he was finally

in front of me.

"Won't you kiss me?" I asked. It seemed like that was all he needed, he took me into his arms and kissed me ardently, making up for the other chaste kisses. Without even asking, he led me to the bedroom and lay me on the bed.

"Forgive me, Kelly, this is going to be quick. I've wanted you for way too long," he said, then stripped off quickly. I watched him sheath his dick with a condom he removed from his pocket, and I smiled. He came towards me and kissed me again, this time a little slowly, just as he removed my underwear. I swatted his hands away and removed it myself, marveling in the expression of sheer delight on his face. James took my nipple into his mouth, kneading at the nub with his teeth before sucking at it. I gasped loudly, and it turned into a shaky moan when two of his fingers found my already wet entrance.

"You're ready for me already, aren't you, princess?" He asked. I preened at the name and gasped out.

"Yes, Daddy," I moaned as James removed his fingers and positioned himself at my entrance, slowly working his way to the hilt. He started out slowly. Then he started thrusting fast, causing my breath to come out in gasps.

"Yes, Daddy. Right there, Daddy," I screamed at the top of my voice as he continued pistoning his dick in and out of my wet hole.

"I'm cumming," I screamed suddenly and wrapped my legs around his waist. A few seconds later, James let out a loud grunt then went limp on top of me.

"Daddy?" I called out. When he didn't respond, I said, "James. Are you listening?"

"Why do you call me, Daddy? Is that some sort of kink?" James asked, after rolling off me. I was silent for some time. I knew this was going to come. I didn't know how to explain it. I didn't want him to be disgusted by me. I bit my lip. Then said a little shyly, "I want you to be my Daddy."

"What exactly do you mean by Daddy?" he asked, looking at me intently. I grew stupidly shy for some reason, so I put down my head. I didn't know how exactly to explain. The words were there, but I was scared to speak because I was in little space. I didn't want to scare him.

"I- Do you know about DDLG?" I asked, enunciating my words slowly so as not to go into little mode.

"I.. I want us to have that. I want you to be my Daddy." I watched him frown a little, then he said, "Can I think about all this?" He asked, clearing his throat. I knew he wasn't going to accept it immediately, but it kind of hurt.

"Okay," I said plainly and turned away. I heard James sigh, then he dressed up, placed a kiss on my forehead, and left.

Chapter 2

James's POV

After I left Kelly, I sat in my car, debating with myself. I didn't know whether to go back to her or just to go home. I finally decided to go home, and I felt like such an asshole. I felt overwhelmed. And I wasn't even sure that this was the right word for it. Kelly had been so sweet. Having her was one of the best things ever. But then she said she was a little. What was that even? And her calling me Daddy? I wasn't too sure if I actually liked it. There could be a lot of things behind the name. And I honestly wasn't sure that I wanted to analyze that. I didn't know how all this made me feel. I hated the fact that I was so weak that I had left Kelly all alone, after sex, vulnerable. But I also didn't want to give her the wrong idea. What if I didn't want this "Daddy" thing? What if I didn't want to be her

Daddy? Staying there was just going to hurt us both more.

I sighed and shifted in my bed. Not only were my balls blue, but my heart also was heavy, and my mind was racing. I wanted to be it for Kelly. But I wasn't ready to accept how the whole thing had made me feel. I sighed and picked up the phone. I knew that she was probably not asleep, so I called her. She picked at the first ring.

"Da– James?" Kelly answered, and my heart warmed up. Kelly was the only person that had succeeded in making me feel this way. I mean, I was 37, the future was all that mattered to me. And I didn't want Kelly's and my future put in peril when we had barely even started.

"Baby girl," I said, wishing that I had not stupidly left.

"I'm sorry for leaving so abruptly," I said and waited for her to reply.

"I– does this mean you're going to come back?" Kelly's voice was hopeful, and I felt bad that I might break her heart.

"I probably shouldn't be saying this, but you're the only person that I want to be my Daddy. James, you're the only person who makes me feel this way. I feel like I can be myself with you. I feel so... loved when I'm with you," Kelly said. I frowned a little. Kelly sounded so vulnerable that I felt like I should go back to her.

"We'll talk about it tomorrow, okay? I'll come over, and we'll talk about it. For now, I want to sleep. Close your eyes. Go to sleep." I said to her, hoping that it would make her feel better.

"Will you stay on the phone with me, James?" Kelly asked innocently, and I shifted uncomfortably in my bed.

"Yes, baby girl, I will. Be a good girl and sleep now," I said, trying to comfort her.

"I love you, Daddy. Goodnight," she replied, making me smile.

"I love you, princess. Sleep tight," I said but stayed on the line until I heard her breathing even out. I felt less guilty now. And I knew that if I hadn't called, she would have spent the whole night agonizing. Now that that was done, maybe it was time for me to sleep as well.

I tried for a couple of minutes, but I just couldn't find a position that was comfortable enough. So I gave up on it. I stared up at the ceiling for some time. Was it wrong that I wasn't ready yet to come to terms with my feelings concerning all this? The Daddy thing and all? All I knew was that Kelly calling me, Daddy, made me feel good about myself. But I didn't want us to rush into something that we weren't ready for. Especially since I didn't have any single notion about this lifestyle.

Yes, she called me Daddy. So what? I thought to myself as I got out of bed and walked to my computer. While it was powering on, I stretched a little and stared into space. I rarely felt out of depth. But right now, without even knowing what I was contemplating getting into, I felt that way. After signing in, I pulled up a tab. And wrote DDLG in the search bar. Just then, I heard a ping sound from my phone. I picked it up and frowned when I saw a message from Kelly. She was supposed to be asleep. The message was just a couple of site links signed with her name and a love emoji. I smiled in spite of myself.

Thank you, princess, now go to bed. Was the message I replied to her with. Without waiting for a response from her, I opened up one of the site links she had sent to me. I took a deep breath and started reading intently, trying not to miss out on any detail.

DD/LG, an acronym for Daddy Dominant/Little Girl in its core, is a kinky age-play/role-play between two consenting adults. I frowned a little then continued scrolling. I wasn't turned off or disgusted, just intrigued. Maybe the disgust was going to come as I read further, but for now, I wanted to know more. All the notions that I had had about the lifestyle were getting dispelled. I didn't know what I was expecting to fall on– some kind of weird incestuous roleplay maybe– but this site specifically stated that there was nothing incestuous about DD/LG. It also stated that the Daddy Dom was the caregiver, and he dominated and disciplined the little while the Little Girl took on a child-like role of a sweet girl, and she regressed in age. A lot of things made sense when I read that. Kelly was often very child-like in her behavior. But I had thought nothing about it, believing that it was in her nature to be that way. Knowing this about her felt comforting. It was hard to imagine how much she had restrained herself with me simply because she didn't want to make me feel uncomfortable. I continued with my reading, marveling at just how many signs I had missed when it came to Kelly. I felt extremely insensitive. And I didn't think anything would help to stop making me feel that way.

I stared blankly at the screen on my phone. After a moment of indecision, I closed up the tab. Kelly and I were going to talk more tomorrow, and we were going to discuss all this. Maybe I was just being a horny old bastard, but the thought of everything about this lifestyle interested me. I got back into bed and stared at the ceiling for a while, a hundred and one thoughts on my mind. I wasn't exactly sure about what I was going to tell Kelly tomorrow. But I had some feeling that it was going to go well. And with thoughts of all that on my mind, I drifted off to sleep.

***

The next morning being a weekend, I woke up pretty early. I had been practicing a doctor for years. Waking up early was a routine for me. Besides, I worked out on weekends, so I needed to be up early. After a hardcore weights workout and a shower, I headed towards Kelly's place. I thought of what to say to her. I didn't know if I should listen to her opinion first before agreeing to anything. I didn't want to raise her hopes high then shatter them. I sighed and parked my car. Granted, all this interested me. I was curious. And it was something I would love to try. But I didn't want my curiosity to end up hurting Kelly. Hurting her was the last thing on my mind. And that was why I wanted us to talk before setting up anything with each other.

I went to her apartment and tried the door. It was open, so I went in, frowning. I had told Kelly numerous times to stop leaving her door open. She was a very beautiful woman. And if anybody with wrong intentions found out that she never locked her door, they might hurt her. I walked in and sighed when I saw that she wasn't even in the living room.

"Kelly?" I called out, removing my coat and hanging it up. It wasn't too chilly outside but cold enough that I needed to wear a coat. This was my favorite type of weather.

"In the bedroom James," she called out. I walked towards the bedroom, and when I reached the door, I started.

"Kelly, how many times have I told you to lock the door? What if an intruder–" words suddenly escaped me. Kelly was standing in front of the mirror, looking completely different from what I was used to. She had her hair up in pigtails. She was wearing an oversized t-shirt which reached her mid-thigh and a pair of thigh-length socks.

"Hi, Daddy. Do you like my outfit?" she asked, smiling cutely at me. I did actually. It was different from what I was expecting to see her in, the usual shorts and cami she wore at home, but I liked it. I held out my hand, and she took it, then we walked to the living room.

"Have you had breakfast?" I asked, pausing a little.

"No, Daddy. I was waiting for you," she said shyly, and I smiled. The fact that she needed me it made me feel powerful and important. It made me feel good, and it made me want to treat her like the princess she was. I was beginning to get with the whole dynamic of this lifestyle. I had forgotten all about the fact that I had had doubts the whole drive over. Seeing Kelly made me happy. Hearing her call me, Daddy, was a special kind of feeling. I wanted to be needed by Kelly. It was a weird realization. But it was true nonetheless.

"Okay, come along. We'll make omelets. You

can help me chop up–" Kelly's laugh interrupted me. It was weird how I had heard her laugh before, but this was different. It sounded like she wasn't holding anything back. And I guess she really wasn't. I liked that she felt she could trust me with this part of herself. I guess some other people would freak out, even more than I had.

"James, I can't be anywhere near a knife. Silly daddy," she said. It was so difficult to associate the vulnerable and sad Kelly to the one who was standing in front of me right now. She looked vibrant, happy, and playful.

"Oh," I said, and she nodded.

"Okay, then you can watch me while I cook, and we'll talk more about this whole thing. How does that sound?" I asked.

"Yes... Daddy, does this mean you are going to be my Daddy? Officially?"

"Yes," I said, beaming despite myself. I couldn't believe how, in just a few short hours, my whole world had turned completely upside down, and I liked it. I saw her eyes get misty, and she hugged me. I held her tight and just enjoyed the feeling of her being in my arms.

"I love you, Daddy. Thank you for agreeing to be my Daddy. I won't ever do anything to displease you. I'll be a good little, I swear. The best little on Earth," she rambled on, and I frowned a little. Looks like someone had hurt my baby girl in the past before.

"We are all humans Kelly. We make mistakes from time to time. And as for agreeing to be your Daddy, I don't regret it. And I won't," I said firmly, as I saw that she was about to protest. I placed a kiss on her forehead and smoothed her hair. Kelly smiled shyly and buried her head in my chest. Then she stood on tippy toes and placed a soft kiss on my mouth. I smiled.

"Now, let's get this breakfast going, shall we?" I asked rhetorically, carrying her up bridal style into the kitchen. Kelly let out a loud squeal, and I laughed. I couldn't help but have this anxious feeling at the back of my mind, though.

"Kelly?" I called, and she answered

absently.

"Did someone hurt you in the past?" I asked, then mentally face palmed myself, disappointed at how insensitive I sounded. I watched as her face shuttered, and I immediately regretted my question.

"Can– can we talk about something else?" she asked. I nodded, then watched her for a moment. I wanted her to open up to me. But I knew I hadn't earned it yet. Until then, I was going to treat her like a queen, just like she deserved.

Kelly's POV

I was lying in James's lap, watching the ceiling. I honestly couldn't explain the feeling that had taken over me when he had said he would be my Daddy. I felt like crying with relief and laughing with joy at the same time. When he had left me all alone after we had sex and after I told him I was a little, I felt so brokenhearted and thought I was going to die. I couldn't even cry. I just felt really empty. When he had called me, though, I didn't want to get too hopeful. His voice had soothed me, even though he technically wasn't giving me what I needed. I didn't know how to explain it, but at that moment, I felt like he needed a push. Maybe I was too forward, but I had gone ahead and sent him links. It worked out eventually, so I didn't regret anything, I guess. And him coming to me the day after to reassure me. It made me feel safe. It made me feel like I was something worth keeping. I felt loved. I felt special.

"James?" I called out.

"Hmm?" James answered, and I smiled. The happiness that came over me every time he answered to me wasn't really something I could explain. It was like I had bared some parts of myself to him, and he hadn't run away or anything. I just felt like jumping on him and screaming to the whole world that he was *my* Daddy, and nobody could take him away from me.

"I just felt like calling you," I said shyly, then buried my head in his chest and inhaled his scent deeply. I honestly didn't know how I was going to survive being apart from him... I really hoped that he stayed with me forever. I knew it was childish of me to have such fairytale thoughts. But it was honestly having them that kept me going. James laughed, and his chest rumbled. It was a nice feeling.

"Baby girl," he called.

"Yes, James," I answered dutifully.

"Sit up now. Let's talk. About all this," he said, and I lifted my head from his chest to look at him. It was interesting how his expressions could change so quickly. From smiling to looking extremely serious.

"Okay, Daddy," I said, but I didn't leave his lap. It was the most comfortable place in the world for me at that moment.

"We need to discuss the whole dynamics of this. The rules. And everything. Don't you think?" James asked, and I nodded dutifully. I knew he needed to put some rules up in place. And I also knew he wasn't too familiar with all this, so I was going to try my best to help him out.

"Okay, we will start with the rules. Rule number–" James began to say.

"Wait for Daddy," I exclaimed excitedly, with a huge smile on my face. The stern look on his face, though, made me quiet down.

"Rule number one, don't interrupt Daddy when he's speaking. We'll let it slide for now. But don't do that again, princess, okay?" He warned with a kiss on my cheek.

"Yes, Daddy," I replied, snuggling into him. There was some silence for a while, and the gloomy look appeared on his face again. Did this mean he no longer wanted to be my Daddy? Was he going to let me go?

"Are you mad at me, Daddy?" I asked in a small voice, not even bearing to look up at his face.

"I'm not mad, Princess. Just thinking," he responded, and I let out a sigh of relief. I lay my head on his chest again and let out another sigh.

"Can we go on with the rules, Daddy?" I said, my voice a little muffled. He was silent again, and I frowned.

"James?" I asked cautiously.

"Don't you think we should talk about all this before getting into the rules?" he asked, and I frowned. I knew exactly what he was hinting at, but I didn't want to give anything away.

"Talk about what?" I asked, pretending not to understand.

"Talk about us. Talk about each other. I don't want this to be an empty relationship with just sex, and you calling me Daddy." I nodded. It was understandable. I knew that sooner or later, I was going to bring up my past. And we had been seeing each other for three months! I felt so comfortable with him, and I genuinely meant it when I said I loved him, but I didn't know if I could talk about what happened.

"Don't shut me out, baby girl. That won't work anymore. Look at me," James said, and I looked up at him. He was right about me shutting him out. I did that often. James placed his hands on both my cheeks and said, "I'm here. I'm going to listen when you're ready. If you don't feel ready, you don't have to say anything, okay?" James explained. I nodded and closed my eyes. I appreciated this man.

"How do you feel about shopping?" James asked, and I perked up.

"I love it!" I exclaimed. It was one of the things that I didn't often do, but it has this therapeutic effect when I do.

"Are you going dressed like that, or do you want to change?" He asked. I paused to look at myself self consciously after James asked that question.

"Do you want me to change? I don't want to embarrass you or anything," I said, scratching at my arm.

"You look beautiful. And you'd never embarrass me," he said and placed a kiss on my forehead. I smiled up at him. It was scary how quickly my walls could fall with James.

Chapter 3

It had been a week since James and I had had sex, and I had confessed to him about me being a little. The week had been pretty fun, with us sneaking as much as we could afford after work, which was very hard. He had spent some nights over at my place, and I was always sad when his beeper had to ring. But it was Saturday again, and hopefully, we were going to spend the whole day together. Without any distractions. I had packed a couple of clothes, and I waited patiently for him to come to pick me up. It was weird just how quickly I was getting really attached to him. But then again, that's how I was.

"Kelly?" James called as he walked into the room. I smiled at him brightly. I stood up and launched myself into his arms, and I felt him laughing.

"Why are you acting like we didn't see each

other in years?" James asked, and I blushed a little.

Did that mean he didn't miss me? I happily thought to myself.

"I.. I just missed you. You didn't miss me?" I asked, rubbing at my arm. I hated when this insecure side of me came out.

"Come here. I missed you," James said making me smile. It felt nice to be appreciated.

"Are you all packed up? Can we leave now?" James asked, and I nodded, standing away from him and rocking on the balls of my feet. I pointed to my bag when he raised a brow. He picked it up and tapped my right butt cheek, and I blushed. We got out, and I locked the door up. We walked to his car in silence. I had so many questions, but I didn't want to annoy him by asking all of them, so I kept quiet. The drive was silent, as well. James kept sneaking looks at me as if he expected me to burst into chatter at any moment. It was the first time I was going over to his place, and I was nervous. When I get nervous, I say stupid shit, so I preferred to keep my mouth shut.

"Why are you so quiet?" James asked, and I blushed a little.

"I don't know.. I'm just nervous," I confided in a small voice. I looked away, then I felt his hand on my lap, stroking it softly.

"You have no reason to be," he said, and I sighed deeply. I knew this. But I couldn't help being paranoid. I was too scared to lose him because of my past. And I couldn't even tell him that because I had been too scared last night to tell him about my past.

"I know. I just..." I sighed again. Then brightened up a little and asked, "What do you have planned?" I asked with a small smile.

"It baffles just how quickly you can bounce back up. I love it," he said, completely avoiding my question. Nevertheless, I blushed at the kind compliment.

"You didn't answer my question," I said, and James laughed.

"It's a surprise," he said and took my hand into his and kissed it. I felt like melting at that instant. This man was everything.

I stayed quiet for the rest of the ride, enjoying the feeling of my hand in his. We reached soon enough, and James opened the door for me. Apparently, I wasn't allowed to. I didn't mind in the slightest, though. It made me feel like a princess. And I told him this.

"You're my princess," James said and placed a kiss on my lips. I sighed when he ended it. Since last week, we hadn't had sex again, no matter how much I had tried to seduce him. I tried not to think about it too much. But I hoped it was going to change this weekend. We got into James' house. It was huge, and I wondered how he's been surviving living there all alone.

"How don't you feel lonely living here all alone?" I asked, looking up at him as he held my hand and led me to the bedroom.

"I'm used to. And you're here now, aren't you?" he asked with a tiny smile. I blushed and grinned widely at him, preferring not to say anything. We got to the bedroom, and when he opened it, I was in awe. His bedroom was big. But that was not what made me happy. In the middle of the room, there was a big bed, and it was filled with all the things a little might need. I turned towards him and looked up with a pleading look on my face.

"Can I Daddy?" I asked, itching to go there already.

"Yes," was all James had to say before I ran there. There were diapers, pacifiers, stuffies, blankies, and so much more. It was like a little heaven. I refrained myself from jumping on the bed, though, tapping my toes until Daddy authorized me to move.

"You don't like them?" his voice came from behind me, and I shook, startled.

"I do, Daddy," I answered, swaying from left to right.

"Then what are you waiting for? You don't want to play with your toys?" He asked, and I smiled big. I placed a kiss on his mouth, then ran to the bed and jumped into it. I picked up one of the stuffies and hugged it to my chest, then dropped it and picked another one. I jumped up excitedly and skipped to Daddy. I placed a kiss on his mouth that he deepened. I sighed when the kiss ended.

"You're the best, Daddy," I said, and I felt his arms tighten around me.

"Now let's change," Daddy said, and I jumped up excitedly. I watched as Daddy packed the things he had gotten me neatly, then he selected a pink onesie from the pile of dresses. He beckoned me to him, and I went obediently. I was wearing a simple t-shirt, jeans and I had already removed my boots. He undressed me gently, stopping once in a while to place kisses on random parts of my body, on my collarbone, on my calf, on my shoulder. At this point, I wanted to just jump into his arms and beg him to take me.

"Lay in my lap, let me put your diaper on," he commanded, and I obeyed. At this point, he could have said, go and fall in the Atlantic and I would have. James spread my legs gently, and I moaned.

"Someone's wet, huh," he said, and I squirmed. I gasped when I felt his fingers parting my pussy lips.

"Daddy," I moaned out as he rubbed my clit.

"You like that?" he asked, and I gasped. One hand was rubbing my clit, and the other was circling my wet hole. I could feel my juices running down my thigh.

"Yes, Daddy, I love it," I gasped out.

"Please, Daddy," I said, unable to bear any more of his teasing. He slid one finger into my wetness, and I sighed deeply. His thrusting was slow at first. Then he added a finger. I let out a gasp. He was still thrusting slowly, and I was rocking my hips to meet his fingers.

"Daddy," I whined, then he added a finger and started thrusting in earnest. It was like he had transported me to seventh heaven. The room was silent, and the only thing you could hear was my loud pants.

"You like that baby girl? Tell me how you like it. I can feel your hole clenching around my fingers," Daddy rasped out, and I moaned.

"I love it, Daddy. Yes, Daddy, right there!" I screamed and clenched my fists tight as the waves of the orgasm crashed over me. I felt his hands on my shoulders, and he made me sit up. I was straddling his laps, and I reached for his zipper. I opened it and removed his already straining erection. I stroked it a little then guided it into my wetness. Both of us sighed as he got into the hilt.

"Ride me, princess," Daddy rasped out. I reached out and held his shoulders, gasping as he bent and took a nipple into his mouth.

"Daddy," I breathed out, rocking my hips slowly at first, then leaning against his chest and moving in up and down movements. Daddy took hold of my face and kissed me. Both of us abandoning all the passion we felt for each other in the kiss. I gasped into the kiss and dug my fingers into his shoulders as a quick orgasm came over me. I felt Daddy jerk into me a few times, then he stilled. We stayed there for a while, him in me, my head on his shoulders. Then he spoke.

"Come, we'll take a bath. Then we'll go over the rules. Deal?" I nodded. I was too tired to argue anyway.

***

"Baby girl?" I heard. I opened my eyes groggily and saw Daddy standing over me. I had probably fallen asleep after the bath. I was dressed, though. The feel of the diaper against my bottom was comforting. It wasn't something I had thought I'd ever feel again.

"Come on. We have to go through the rules now," he said, and I rubbed my eyes sleepily. I sat up and watched him open his drawer. He removed a slightly thick pile of papers, and I widened my eyes.

"Are you hungry?" he asked, and after thinking for a while, I nodded. Daddy came with a feeding bottle and sat me in his lap. I stared up at him as he fed me, wondering what I had done to deserve such a loving Daddy. When I was done, he removed the bottle and wiped my mouth. We settled in, and he picked up what I presumed was the rules and contract.

"Daddy, are we going to read all this?" I asked in surprise. I really didn't want to.

"I want you to read all of it. I'll give you time to do that obviously. And when you're done, you tell me what you don't agree with. Deal?" Daddy said, and I sighed a little.

"You'll stay here with me, won't you, Daddy?" I asked, looking up at him with a pleading expression on my face. I smiled when he nodded, and I opened the to the first page. It was written boldly, OUR DDLG RELATIONSHIP. I started reading, and most of it was just explaining what everything meant. I smiled. Daddy had done a lot of research to make sure everything went well. I continued reading. Then I looked up at him.

"Daddy, I have an issue," I said, and he came to my side.

"What's that, baby girl?" Daddy asked, looking down at the contract.

"The duration.. it says 'indefinite' instead of 'forever,'" I said, then stuck out my tongue to make it known I was joking. He laughed and sat behind, pulling me into his chest. I kept on reading, paying more attention when I reached the rules I was supposed to follow. They were pretty easy.

Rules

1. No cussing
2. Always talk to Daddy if there's something wrong
3. Before making purchases that aren't really essential, check-in with Daddy
4. Never lie to Daddy
5. Be polite and respectful to everyone, especially Daddy.
6. Get at least six hours of sleep every night
7. Respect each rule, or you'll get punished
8. Don't touch yourself without Daddy's permission
9. If you break a rule, talk Daddy.

I was okay with these rules. So I looked up at

Daddy.

"Where do I sign Daddy?" I asked, looking up at him.

"Are you sure there's nothing you'd like to change, baby girl?" he asked, and I shook my head. I trusted Daddy. Maybe not as much as he would love me too. I took the pen he stretched at me and signed. When he took everything from me, I sat up suddenly. I had forgotten to talk to him about something! Mostly because I wasn't very sure that he was going to accept to be my Daddy.

"Daddy?" I called, and he let out a grunt in response.

"Well, there's this kink party next week. I was wondering if you'd like to go with me?" I asked, hoping he would say yes. I closed my eyes and waited for his response. I really didn't want to hear a no.

"Sure, baby girl. When is it?" He asked.

"Next weekend, Daddy," I replied.

"You really want to go?" James asked, and I nodded frantically.

"Alright then, Princess." I squealed excitedly and kissed him.

"You won't regret it, Daddy," I assured him. It was going to be fun. It was on Saturday. Daddy and I reached the venue a little late. But that was because my diaper had gotten wet and he had to change it. But it wasn't really a problem. I just wanted to have some fun with James. As soon as we got in, I spotted most of my friends sitting in one corner, and I fought the urge to squeal. I hadn't seen any of them in a while since I didn't have anyone to be my Daddy. Daddy walked us up to a group of Daddies were sitting. I knew all of them, but I was shy. I looked down and stood behind Daddy partially. I didn't really want to be the center of attention.

"Are you with Kelly?" one of them asked, and I blushed. The blushed intensified even more when Daddy affirmed this.

"Sure do hope you treat her right after what that bastard did to her." One of the other men said. Daddy and I tensed at the same time. But he didn't ask them any questions, and I was grateful for that. I wanted to tell him myself. I turned towards my friends and saw some of them waving at me. I squealed and hid my face behind James's back.

"Do you want to go play with your friends Kelly?" Daddy asked, and I nodded frantically.

"Go ahead," he said, and I skipped off.

"Is that your new Daddy?" Reese, one of my friends asked.

"Yes," I responded shyly, "He's the best Daddy ever."

"Is he better than you know who?" Reese asked again, and I nodded. My previous Daddy had been a horrible person. But James was nothing like that. At that, all of us turned towards our Daddies and watched them. They seemed to be in an engaging conversation. So we turned back to each other and started talking.

"Oh my God, my Daddy punished me in public, and I really liked it," Francie, one of my louder friends said after a while of us discussing, and we all gasped. All of a sudden, I wanted that. I wanted Daddy to punish me.

***

"Daddy, I'm home!" I call from the front door. When I got home from work and saw Jame's car in the driveway, I was so excited that he was home early, I ran up the garden path and quickly opened the door. But I knew he wouldn't have heard me come in because I heard the shower running. I put my bag down on my special pink bag hook in his mudroom and kicked my wet boots off, placing them on the shoe rack just the way he liked. I like that I can do the things that Daddy taught me without him needing to remind me to do them. Sometimes I really love being his good girl, today felt like one of those days. I giggle as I tiptoe to the bathroom, hearing him singing in the shower. I've never had a Daddy who sings in the shower before, and I sit by the door and listen to his songs. James is a surprisingly good singer. I was surprised when he first sang for me in the car ride home from our first picnic in the woods. I had pressed the window down, my hair getting windswept as I felt the air against my face, and he turned the radio down and began to sing. His song, making me blush and unsure of what to do as I sat quietly in my seat and listened. He looked at me several times during it, making me uncertain of what to say, so I just settled in and let him reach me with his song. I've gotten used to him suddenly bursting out in song since then.

I've even found myself missing it when he's had a big day and doesn't have a song in his heart.

"Oh, little girl, I didn't hear you come in," James says opening the door suddenly. I giggle, and he bends down to kiss me before taking my hand and leading me to the bedroom.

"How was your day?" He asks, making me roll my eyes. I hate talking about my day with anyone else but Thea. Especially with doctors. They think they are the most important people at the hospital, and even though James isn't like that, I'd rather not talk about my day with him.

"Lame," I reply, not interested in telling him

about my boring day filled with boring people who lead boring lives. He smiles, and I can see he has other things on his mind as well.

"Why don't you come here," he says, patting his lap as he sits down on the edge of the bed. I bite my bottom lip, surprised that he'd want to give me a random spanking but move to him as instructed. I hold my breath as I lay across his lap.

"Lift up your skirt," James whispers, making my heart race as I reach behind and expose my emerald green lace thong. I can tell he likes it by the way his hands move over my firm, full ass, feeling my wetness as he pushes my thighs apart.

"Such a pretty little girl," he says, patting my ass. James holds my head in the nook of his arm as I tense my thighs on his lap and fight my urge to snuggle into him. I know that he isn't finished with his fun by the way he is running his finger up and down my wet, panty-covered slit. I suck my bottom lip, only for him to replace it with his thumb, correcting me when I slowly stink my teeth into it for fun.

"If you have to much energy, I'll give you something else to do," he says, making me try to hide my smirk. He pulls my panties to the side and continues his slow onslaught, making me whimper in frustration. He was waiting for that. I know how he likes me on edge, begging for his touch.

"No, you're not there yet," he casually says, continuing to tease me. I want to have more of him, as I slightly buck my hips, wanting him inside of me.

"Don't be such a slut. You'll get what I give you," he says, making me groan in frustration. Suddenly, he enters me with two fingers, curling them inside of me and stroking up and down my arching back.

"My little gymnast," he says as I stuck on his thumb and push my hips down on his hand.

"Come on, then, come and get it," he says, taking his thumb from my mouth and wrapping his arm around my neck as he pushes into me firmly, making me take him hard and fast.

"Don't make me wait," he whispers. I know

what I'm supposed to do as I begin backing up onto his hand, grinding down on the fingers he has filled me with as his thumb begins to rub my clit, making me moan.

"Good girl," he says, standing up and watching as I catch myself before I hit the ground.

"Just like a little pussy cat," James says, watching as my body contorts, the muscles of my toned arms, tummy, and thighs flexing in the subtle light coming from that hallway lamp. I move to stand in front of him, unsure of what he wants me to do before he smiles and reaches out for my hand, pulling me to him.

Chapter 4

James's POV

Kelly woke me up with her screams. I took her into my arms and soothed her until she woke up. Then I frowned. She looked really scared, and the tears on her cheeks told me this was really bad.

"Hey, baby. Want to talk about it?" I asked, smoothing her hair down. Last night at the kink party had gone so well. Kelly had behaved decently, and I had made new friends that were also into this lifestyle. So I didn't understand what had provoked the nightmare and screaming.

"I. No. Yes, Daddy. Please," Kelly said, and I sat up completely in bed.

"Wait, before that. Let's check your diaper," I said, and she laid her face down with her butt facing me. I opened up her onesie, and when I checked her diaper, it was still dry. I buttoned up the onesie again and sat her up again.

"Ready to talk now?" I asked, and Kelly nodded. After some silence, she started, "I had a Daddy before you. His name was Alex. I met him when I was 20, and he introduced me to this lifestyle. We were together for three years." I watched her as she spoke, wishing I could take all the pain from her little body. She continued, "He was good to me at first. He was really caring and had my best interests at heart. I really loved him. And I thought he loved me too." I clenched my palms at the thought of her loving someone else, but I didn't interrupt Kelly. I could tell from her demeanor that she really needed to pour out everything.

"Then he became really controlling, way more than a Daddy should. He would try to stop me from going to the hospital and punish me each time I had a night shift even though it wasn't my fault." I fought the urge to punch something. So I just took Kelly's face into my hands and placed a soft kiss on her forehead, then urged her to continue.

"He would stop me from doing things, from seeing my friends. We stopped going to kink parties together, and he basically cut me off from the rest of the world. And he kept on reminding me that I was useless and that he was the only Daddy in the world who could tolerate me. Because I was such a bad little.

"He would play with my feelings. Bring other littles home and play with them in front of me. He wanted to break me, and he was succeeding slowly. Then the beatings started. They were no longer punishments. I had bruises everywhere, and I became ashamed of my body and wore heavy makeup and clothes to cover my whole body. My friends grew worried about me. And Kyle, who is a police officer, was able to get me away from him. I filed a restraining order against him, and I've never seen him since then," Kelly explained to me. I was sure I looked distraught at hearing the life she had lived in the past.

It was silent, then I asked, trying to control the barely restrained fury that was begging to come out, "Is that what made you have the nightmare?"

"Yes, Daddy. I dreamt that he came back and that he hurt you really bad," Kelly said and started sobbing. I pulled her into my arms and placed kisses everywhere I could reach while whispering reassurance into her ears. When the sobs subsided, I lifted her face and said seriously, "Princess, you are more than enough. You are one of best things that has ever happened to me, and I wouldn't trade you for anything in this world. And don't worry, that dickhead is part of the past, and he will remain there, okay?" I said seriously. Kelly nodded, then leaned forward and placed a kiss on my lips.

"I love you, Daddy," she said.

"I love you too, princess. Now let's go to sleep," I said and placed one last kiss on her forehead. I had a hard time falling asleep because of all the pent up rage. I hated men like that, ones who used their power to prey on others, especially the women they were supposed to protect. I looked at Kelly, who had already fallen asleep, and I placed a kiss on her lips and tried to fall asleep as well.

***

A week later, I went over to Kelly's place. I was really contemplating asking her to move in with me, and it would make things way easier, but I was scared she was going to think everything was going too quick. And I honestly wasn't sure I was ready either. I got into her apartment as her door was still unlocked. I walked into her bedroom, preparing to scold her, but she hid something from me and looked at me with a defiant look on her face. Okay this was definitely not what I was expecting to find

"What are you hiding?" I asked calmly, and Kelly shook her head. I frowned.

"Kelly, what are you hiding?" I asked again, and she shook her head again. I advanced towards her and changed my tone into a stern one.

"Don't make me ask again, Kelly. What are you hiding?" I asked in a stern voice.

"It's none of your business!" Kelly exclaimed, and I couldn't help the shock that came over my features. Kelly had never been disrespectful to me. This was a first.

"What did you just say?" I asked, narrowing my eyes.

"I said, James, it's none of your business," she repeated, rolling her eyes. I looked at her in shock. She was casually breaking the rules and rolling her eyes at that. Being completely disrespectful to me. I walked to her and picked her up easily. What I saw made me even more disappointed.

"Kelly, what was rule number 3," I asked lowly, looking down at the Nintendo on her bed. I had bought the exact one for her, and it was still at my home, so I didn't understand why she had purchased another one.

"No unnecessary purchases without letting

Daddy know," she said in a small voice. Good. She was getting remorseful.

"And what is this?" I asked, looking at her.

"A Nintendo 3DS XL," she mumbled.

"And what did I get you just last week?" I asked patiently, my eyes never leaving her face.

"A Nintendo 3DS XL," she said, and before I could speak, Kelly rushed to justify herself.

"Daddy, I was really bored, and I had forgotten it over at your place. I just wanted to play with something," she explained with tears already in her eyes. Her explanation was meaningful, and I wanted just to let her off the hook. But I knew that I had to punish her because she had broken the rules — two, to be more precise.

"You know I'm going to punish you now, right?" I asked, setting her on the bed and picking up the Nintendo.

"Firstly, you're not going to use this for a while. Then I am going to spank you. You will count out each spank, and at the end, you'll tell me why I punished you and tell me if you think it was justified." I walked towards her and almost caved in when she looked up at me with teary eyes. But I hardened my resolve and put her in my lap after I sat. I bared her bottom and rubbed her ass. I lifted my arm, and I was about to give her the first spank, memories flashed in my mind. I closed my eyes and tried to forget them. I lifted my arm again and placed the first spank on her ass.

"One," Kelly screamed out. I lifted my arm again to give her the second spank, but I found that I was unable to. The flashbacks were deafening.

"Dad, please stop hurting Mom!" a really younger James screamed, holding his father's arm. The latter jerked his arm and sent James flying...

"Promise me you'll never hurt a woman. Promise me. You won't ever make a woman suffer like your father made me suffer. Promise me, James," a frail woman said, holding the hand of her young son.

This one was sobbing as he said, "I promise."

I shook my head suddenly and came back to the present. I saw Kelly there with her bum exposed and me about to hit it. After my promise to my mother. I quickly buttoned her onesie, placed her on the bed, and stood up. I couldn't do it.

"Daddy?" Kelly asked, the confusion in her voice apparent.

"I'll be back," I said and left the house as if I had the devil chasing me.

***

I had called up Kyle, Ryan, and David, the other Daddy Doms I had met at the kink party. We had stayed in touch, and they were incredibly helpful at any time I needed help. So I called them for a drink. I didn't know what to do anymore. And once again, like a coward, I had left Kelly all alone. I knew that aftercare was extremely important. And I could just imagine how she was feeling at home all alone, with the person she called Daddy not even present to comfort her.

"Hey, man," Kyle said. He was staring at me, curiously. I sighed. It hadn't even been a full day since the whole spanking thing, and I was sure I already looked like crap.

"Hey man," I returned his greeting, then picked up my glass of whiskey again and shook it in the glass. Just at the moment, David and Ryan entered. They both frowned when they spotted me.

"What's wrong, man?" It was David, and I sighed.

"It's that obvious, isn't it?" I said tiredly.

"You look like shit," this time around, it was Ryan. I sighed and buried my hand in my hair, then raked it through. I was a mess. They stared at me for a while, presumably waiting for me to tell them why I had called them here. I started hesitantly.

"Have you, have you ever had a hard time spanking your little?" I asked. I fully expected them to burst into laughter, but all they did was stare at me with worry.

"What happened?" David asked. I explained

what had happened, and Ryan let out a whistle.

"So your past won't let you discipline her?" he asked, and I nodded miserably.

"I want to be the best Daddy I can be to Kelly. And I know punishing her when she does wrong is one of the steps. But how do I do that when I keep being such a fucking headcase." I said, looking miserable.

"Hey man, take it easy. It mustn't be easy on you either. And you stressing about it isn't going to make it any better. Maybe you should talk to Kelly. She's a sweet girl. She'll understand," Kyle said. The others nodded in agreement and I looked at them before sighing.

"Thank you for your help," I replied. Speaking with the guys had genuinely made me feel better. It had made me feel good, telling them my problem, but I doubted I was going to follow that piece of advice. I didn't want Kelly to see that fucked up part of me yet. I knew it was unfair since she had already confided in me. But I guess I just wasn't ready.

"Thanks, guys," I said as we all made to leave. We had spent a little more time with each other, and I couldn't say I regretted it. I got into my car and drove towards Kelly's house.

I removed the key she had given me and used it to open the door. It was already dark, so I knew she was probably asleep since it was already weekend. I walked to the bedroom quietly. I undressed and walked to the bed softly. I put on the night lamp for a bit, and my heart broke when I saw the tear tracks on her cheeks. I turned it off because I couldn't bear the sight any longer. I slid into the bed and gathered her into my arms.

"I'm sorry, princess. I love you," I whispered and kissed her forehead and smoothed her hair. I silently swore to myself that it was the last time I was going to try to spank her. I was going to be better than her no-good former Daddy.

"Daddy? Is that you?" She called out sleepily.

"Yes, it's me. Sleep now, baby," I said. I held

her like that until I fell asleep.

Chapter 5

Kelly's POV

For some time, it was like James had been avoiding me. I knew he had work. I had work too. I knew he was busy. But every time I called him, he made up some excuse. I felt so hurt. I didn't know what I had done wrong. And I really wanted to know so I could work on it. Or was it that he had gotten tired of me and couldn't bear to be my Daddy any longer? Because I was honestly quite tired of waiting like this with no contact at all with him. I mean yes, I had Thea and my other friends from the kink parties. But it just wasn't the same. There were some things I could talk to James about that I couldn't tell anyone else. And there were lots of things I was itching to tell him. But he wasn't available. And that made me sad, so I made up a plan. I was going to pay him a surprise visit at the hospital. He would have no choice but to talk to me and tell me exactly what I had done wrong. I went to his hospital after my shift and walked to the lobby. The hospital was big. But I had been there before, so I knew my way through it. I walked to the pediatric section, which I knew was where James was.

There was an older woman standing behind a desk. I walked to her and asked, "Hi. Is Dr. James Saunders still on duty?" I was polite, so I fully expected her to answer the question. I wasn't prepared for the nasty look she gave me before asking, "And who would you be?" I had changed out of my scrubs, so I looked down at my body to see if there was anything amiss. But I couldn't find anything to warrant her mean look.

"I'm his fiancé," I said, obviously lying. But I knew if I said anything else, she wouldn't give me the time of day and I really needed this to work.

"Well, if you were his fiancé, you'd know if he were or duty or not, wouldn't you?" the woman asked with a smug smile on her face. I sighed and stared at her.

"I don't know his schedule. And he's a doctor. It changes. So even if I did know what his schedule looks like, I can't guarantee I'm right."

"Look ma'am–" she started but was interrupted by James.

"What's going on here?" he asked in his deep voice staring at both of us. I was tempted to run towards him and hug him, but at this point, I wasn't even sure about the reception he would give me. And I didn't want to be embarrassed in front of the rude receptionist.

James crooked his finger at me with a puzzled look on his face, and I went towards him. I hugged him and took in his scent.

"Oh, Doctor James, I apologize. I thought she was just lying when she said she was your fiancé," the receptionist said with a sheepish look on her face. I fought the urge to stick my tongue out at her. I was getting mature.

"It's okay. Next time you answer her questions," he said and muttered a small "let's go" to me. We walked out, and he led me to the parking lot. It was all very silent, and I honestly didn't know what to say at this point. I mean, I had burning questions on my mind. But I didn't want to ridicule myself. I wasn't going to force myself on someone who didn't want me.

"Fiancé, huh," he said as he started the car and started driving towards his house.

"I didn't want our hidden relationship to be exposed, but you gave me no choice," I said with a nonchalant shrug. I didn't even look at him.

"Hidden relationship? That's how you feel?" James asked, and I shrugged my shoulders again. Maybe coming here was a bad idea. But I just wanted to see my Daddy.

"Look at me when I'm talking to you," he said, and I pretended not to hear him. My head was turned towards the window, and I was looking blankly out of the window.

"Kelly," he called.

"Yeah," I answered after a short while. I aimed to provoke him. I was going to break all the rules in such a way that he would have no choice but to become my true Daddy and give me a punishment. I looked at him through the corner of my eye and saw that his fists were clenched tight on the steering wheel. Good. He was getting mad. I decided to up everything a little.

"Daddy?" I said.

"Yes, Kelly," he said, and it was so obvious that he was pissed. First of all, he never called me Kelly. And secondly, he was clenching his teeth so hard that I was scared they were going to break.

"I. You said to tell you when I broke a rule, right?" I asked as innocently as I could.

"Yes, I did. What did you do?" James asked, and I could tell that he had managed to get some of his anger under control. The devil side of me wanted to spark it up again and make it even worse.

"I... yesterday, I touched myself, Daddy. It was so fucking good. And besides, there was no one else to do it for me," I said with a sad sigh.

"Where did you touch yourself?" he asked, and I smiled to myself. I like that he actually cared.

"At the hospital, Daddy," I said, pretending to misunderstand him.

"You touched yourself at the hospital?" He asked, and I almost dropped the act and told him that I had been a good girl.

"Yes, Daddy. I did. I'm sure everyone could smell how wet my pussy was." I replied. I was going to break all those rules today. He should just watch and see. James stopped the car and stared at me for a while. Without saying anything, he started the car again and practically flew us to his house. My heart was beating so fast, and I let out a sigh of relief when we reached, and he parked in the garage. As soon as I got out of the car, he came to me and took my hand, dragging me into the house.

"Let me go!" I exclaimed, dragging my feet on the floor. James didn't even make as if he was listening to me. Just continued dragging me. I dug in my steps and refused to move anymore. And that was when he picked me up like a sack of potatoes and put me over his shoulders. I started screaming and kicking, shouting out obscenities. He walked to the bedroom and dumped me on the bed. I sat up and looked at him. He didn't do anything to me, just started walking up and down in the room. I was incredulous. I have provoked him so badly, and all he was going to do was make a hundred steps around the room? I was frustrated at this point. I didn't know what to do next, so I picked up my sippy cup from where it usually stood and threw it at him. He stopped and stared at me with surprise on his face. I took a stuffie this time around and aimed right for his stupid perfect face.

"Kelly stop," James said, but I paid him no mind. I kept throwing things at him. I wanted a reaction. I wanted it now.

"I hate you," I said lowly, then I started screaming it. "I hate you, I hate you, I hate you, I hate–" I was cut off by James kissing me.

"You hate me, huh?" he said, and I

swallowed.

Was he going to punish me now? I thought a slight panic flowed through my body making my eyes go wide. What he did next shocked me. He took hold of my shirt and tore it. I looked at him with wide eyes. I was wearing a short rayon skirt, and he couldn't tear that, so he just dragged it down a little roughly. He tore my bra and my panties as well, then spread my legs in a jerky movement.

"You hate me, huh?" he asked again in a tone I couldn't place. He had never been this way with me, and I was surprised and turned on at the same time.

"I hate you," I whispered, not even sure of what I was saying anymore. He knelt in front of the bed, and his tongue brushed my clit. I almost screamed, but I held it in.

"You hate it when I do this?" he asked, then before I could answer, his tongue went back to my clit. This time it did more than kiss it. He laved hungrily at it, and I couldn't help but moan out.

Then his fingers found my already wet and pulsating hole. He started off right away with two fingers, and I screamed when he started thrusting them into my wet heat. He lifted his head from my clit.

"You like that you little slut, you like my fingering your pussy, huh? Look how wet and messy you are. I can feel your hole clenching around my fingers," he said. I couldn't even say a word. I just kept on moaning and clutching at his head. He bent again and removed his finger, sending his tongue directly into my hole. He thrust it in and out of me like it was a little erection. I was writhing on the bed. I placed both my hands on his head and started lifting my lips to meet his tongue.

"Yes, Daddy. Please, Daddy," I screamed, riding his tongue. I screamed as my orgasm came over me. When I came down from my high, I was panting loudly, and my legs were still shaking. I watched James stand up and approach me. He held my face in his hand and looked at me, then kissed me. I responded immediately. There was no fight for dominance because we already knew who had won. When the kiss ended, he said, "Do you still hate me?" I looked away.

How could I even hate him? I thought as I rolled my eyes and kissed him again.

Chapter 6

"Can we talk now? You don't hate me anymore?" James asked, and I sighed. We were in bed, and he was behind me, we were spooning. I wasn't wearing a thing, and neither was he. I could feel his erection on my ass, but I wasn't going to let it distract me. We had to have a serious conversation.

"I don't hate you, James. I'm sorry about my behavior. I'm just baffled. I thought you wanted this. I don't want you to feel as if I'm forcing you to be my Daddy," I confessed, holding on to the arm that was on my boobs. James was silent for some time, and I sighed a little. I wanted this to work out. I didn't want to come off as that little that was too pushy or anything. I had already been in a bad relationship before. I didn't want another one. Because I didn't think I would be able to survive the heartbreak.

"I want this, Princess. I want it as much as you do, maybe more. I need you. I need you needing me. I need you wanting me. I never want it to end. But I just have so many things on my mind," he explained, and I frowned.

"Things on your mind?" I turned with difficulty so our eyes could meet. I found it better to communicate when I could see the emotions that were crossing his face.

"My past. My past keeps me from doing all this with you," Daddy said. He sounded so sad that I felt my heart break a little. I put my small hand on his face and smoothed it.

"Daddy, you can talk to me. I'm your little. We have to trust each other, remember?" I reminded him then placed a kiss on his cheek.

"I know this baby girl," was all he said. I waited and looked at him. His eyes were closed, and his Adam's apple moved as he swallowed. I didn't want to push him. I wanted to give him the same respect he had given me. I loved him. But it was hard because seeing him like this was killing me. I wanted to do something to make him feel better. And I knew that him talking about whatever was bothering him would be a good start.

"My father hit my mother," Daddy started. I looked up at him with surprise in my eyes. His eyes were still closed. It was almost like he didn't want me to *see* him if that made sense.

"He started after her first miscarriage. I was seven at the time. I was way too young, even to understand what a miscarriage was. And too young to defend the woman who had put me in this world." I took James's hands into mine and kissed them. My heart reached out to him, and I felt so sad that he had to experience something like that at such a young age.

"He apologized and all that. Said he'd never do it again. It was frustration, he said. But I saw my mother wither. She was never the same. Then he hit her again. I was ten this time. I was older. But what could a ten-year-old boy do against a robust man in his forties?

"He would do it repeatedly until it became a routine. My mother was late for work. He hit her. My mother made his food late. He hit her. His food was cold. He hit her. He found every excuse to hit her," James said as his lip was sneered in disgust, and I wanted just to hold him forever. I felt so sad that I couldn't do anything just to make him better instantly, even though I knew that things didn't work like that.

"Then my mother announced she was pregnant. I was twelve by this time. Things got better. He stopped hitting my mother. He treated her like an egg. She wasn't to do anything at home. And if she did, he scolded her. He urged her to quit her job, pretending that the stress was going to be too much for her to bear. And for a while, it actually seemed like things were looking up.

"Then my mother lost the baby. Everything went downhill from there. He came back home from the hospital in a rage. He locked me up in my closet. I didn't know how much time I spent there. I was let out sometime after by a neighbor. She drove me to the hospital. The looks she kept on giving me were telltale of something bad happening.

"Without even asking, I knew it was my mother. When I got to the hospital, she was laying there in bed. She looked like a shell. She looked very weak. And tired. But she smiled at me. And told me to come to her. I started crying. I didn't even know how I knew it. But I knew she wasn't going to make the night.

"She asked me one thing only. She asked me to promise never to hit a woman. I remember her exact words. They will never leave my mind. That night when I was supposed to punish you, I couldn't. I kept on thinking about her. And I kept on thinking of what she would say if she witnessed me in a position like that," James explained. He was silent after that. He opened his eyes, and I could see the tears glistening. I reached out impulsively and kissed his chin.

"Daddy," I said, then I hugged him. I knew he wasn't going to cry. But seeing him so emotionally weak killed me.

"Daddy, I'm sorry that happened to you. And I love you even more after hearing this. But Daddy.you said you needed me to need you, right? I need you to do this. I need you to punish me. When I do wrong, you correct me. It makes me feel loved. I feel loved when you correct me for my wrongdoings. Think of it that way. I'll understand if you still don't want to." I didn't even know if I had made sense at all. But Daddy kissed me then hugged me even tighter to him. That was how we fell asleep, hugging to each other.

***

I woke up the next morning. Then I panicked. It was Thursday. I was supposed to be at work. I looked at the bedside clock and saw that it was almost ten in the morning. In a panic, I jumped out from the bed and ran to the bathroom. After brushing my teeth, I took a quick shower then I stopped. What was I going to wear? James had torn my clothes yesterday. And it would be so strange for me to walk in with men's clothes. Or with a onesie. I didn't think I could bear the eyes of everyone of me when I got out of the car. I tied a towel around my body and went in the search for James. I found him in the kitchen, making breakfast.

"Daddy? Why didn't you wake me up? I'm late for work, and I have nothing to wear," I complained, walking towards him.

"Baby, don't worry about that. You're not going into work today. Or tomorrow. I called in sick for you," he said, and I widened my eyes. Was this man, okay?

"Why?" I asked, confused.

"We're going on a vacation. We're going to Hawaii," he exclaimed with a smile. I squealed. "For real Daddy?" I exclaimed.

"Yes, Princess. For real," he said, and I jumped up into his arms. My towel slipped. I widened my eyes then looked at him through my lashes.

"Don't give me that look, Missy. If you don't want me to bend you over and slide right into your wetness, you'd better go the bedroom and wait for me to dress you.

"Yes, Daddy," I said coyly and giggled as he slapped my ass as I ran to the room. I sat dutifully and waited for him, playing with my stuffies. I looked up when he got into the room, and I smiled happily.

"Daddy!" I exclaimed then lifted my arms.

"Princess," Daddy said with a smile, and I giggled. He lifted me and put me on his lap. He kissed me then placed me on the bed. I watched as he went to the drawers and pulled out a onesie, sockies, and a diaper. Then he came and popped my paci into my mouth, and I started sucking on it. After he changed me successfully, he carried me to the dining table. There was a high chair for me already, so he made me sit there and put food in front of me. He removed the pacifier from my mouth and placed it on a clean tissue. Then he tied a bib around my neck. I loved Daddy feeding me, so I gave him the puppy eyes until he sat and started feeding me.

"Good girl. You aren't too messy," he said when he was done feeding me. I preened at the praise and smiled up at him. He went ahead and put me on a mat in the living room with my toys, a blankie, and my sippy cup on it. I started playing, but then I got bored and held my blankie to me. I wanted to sleep. I must have actually fallen asleep because the next thing I knew, Daddy was waking me up to come to the car.

"Daddy? Where are we going?" I asked, rubbing at my eyes.

"Stop rubbing your eyes. You're going to hurt them. And we are going to the airport," he responded. I let him carry me, and I snuggled into his arms. He put me in the car and put my seatbelt on with a pillow under my head. I fell asleep again. I had no recollection of how everything happened, but the next thing I knew, I was on a bed, and Daddy was sleeping behind me. I frowned. Had we already reached? I hadn't slept that long.

"Daddy," I whispered. I shook him a little and watched as his nose twitched when he woke up.

"Yes, Princess," he answered groggily.

"Where are we?" I asked in a hushed voice.

"On the plane, baby girl," he answered, and I frowned. I thought we were going to take a commercial flight? I asked him.

"No, baby. A friend of mine gave me this as a loan," Daddy explained then said, "Go to sleep Princess." My mouth was still wide open, but I forced myself to lay next to Daddy. Thea was still bugging me about the $150 I had borrowed from her when we were in nursing school. And my Daddy's friends gave him planes to borrow. Wow. It must be nice to be that rich.

***

We reached sometime after and I was so excited. We were in a very beautiful house that had its own private beach, and I just couldn't wait to explore everything. Daddy had packed up everything, including bikinis. He had bought them, though, because they still had tags on, so we changed and headed down to the beach. I was running up and down, and I ignored Daddy when he told me to slow down. I kept on running all over the place. And every time I saw a shell, I stopped to pick it up.

"Slow down, Princess," I heard again, but I pretended not to hear. All of a sudden, a wave crashed into me, and the force of it almost pulled me in. When it finally receded, I saw another wave. But this time, it was in the form of a human. Daddy had a thunderous look on his face as he walked towards me.

"Come. We'll see whether you will disobey again after this," Daddy said, and I widened my eyes. Did this mean he was going to punish me? I swallowed. Instead of being scared, I was kinda excited. We walked to the house in silence, and I could feel the anger coming off Daddy in waves. We reached the bedroom, and he said, "Remove your bottoms." I obeyed and waited for the next command.

"Come. Lay in my lap," Daddy said, sitting on the bed. I walked to him and did as he said.

"Now I'm going to give you twenty spanks. Ten for putting your life in danger. And then for not listening to me, you'll get another ten. You count out each. If you don't, we'll start all over." James had a slight grin on his face, and it made me wonder if he was actually feeling better about spanking me or if he was just pretending. I swallowed and closed my eyes, waiting for the impact. It didn't come when I expected it to. But I flinched in pain. Daddy had to spank me again to remind me to start counting. By the time we reached ten, the tears were already going down my eyes. I didn't want to cry out loud tho. I didn't want Daddy to think I was hurting and stop the punishment. When we reached twenty, Daddy immediately pulled me up, and his expression got sad when he saw my tears.

"Are you okay?" he asked, sounding

concerned. I loved it that he always checked to make sure that everything was still fine. I smiled and kissed his thigh.

"Yes, Daddy. Thank you for punishing me," I said. He stood up with me in his arms and walked to the bathroom. He ran a bath and undressed me totally. When the bath was ready, he put me in it and washed me thoroughly, making sure to remind me that he loved me and that he was punishing me for my own good.

"I love you, Daddy," I said when he kissed my shoulder for like the hundredth time.

"I love you too, Princess. Don't ever forget," he said, and I misted up a little. Then he got into the bath with me. We stayed there until the water got cold. Then we got out. Then we went to the bedroom and cuddled in bed. I closed my eyes and just enjoyed the feel of his body against mine without anything sexual attached to it.

Chapter 7

After the weekend, I hadn't heard from Daddy. He had dropped me off at my place, kissed me hard, and passionately then told me to be "a good girl." I was so confused because his words sounded final and loving at the same time. I didn't know what to make of it. But now, here we were, a day later, and I hadn't heard from him. This was getting annoying. We were fine one day and then the next, he just ghosted me. It wasn't a very nice feeling. I was lonely. Yes I had friends. But Thea wasn't into the lifestyle so she wouldn't understand. And my other friends who were actually littles would just tell me to be patient. Their daddies were always there, so they didn't know how it felt to be lonely like this. Maybe I was being dramatic because it was just a day. But I needed attention. And Daddy was the only person who knew how to give me the kind of attention I wanted.

When I got back home from work, I received a call from him, and it put me right into a good mood. He told me he was busy and that he was going to make the effort of coming over the next day. I was sad he wasn't going to come at that instant. But I felt relieved that he didn't want to leave me. These abandonment issues weren't things you got rid of in one day. I got another call. From an unknown number. I frowned. But I picked it up. It could be important.

"Hello?" I said hesitantly, hoping it wasn't Alex or something.

"Kelly?" The person said. The voice sounded vaguely familiar, but I couldn't place it.

"Yes. This is Kelly. Who's speaking, please?" I asked, hoping the person didn't get offended and hang up or something. Trust me. It had happened to many times to count to me.

"It's Olivia," was the reply. I frowned, then my eyes widened in realization. I had met Olivia when I had just gotten with Alex. We had gotten along very well, and we told each other everything. But she had to move with her Daddy, and that was when we stopped communicating with each other.

"Oh my God, it's been like five years," I exclaimed.

"Not that long. But yeah," she said, laughing.

"How have you been?" Olivia asked, and I smiled.

"I've been good babes. And you?" I asked.

"Not too good," she replied.

"Oh, why," I asked, worried. I mean, we hadn't spoken to each other in years. But she was still my friend and friendship didn't die off, even if communication died off.

"I.. can we meet up and talk? Like right now?" Olivia asked, and the sadness in her voice made my heart break a little. I loved Olivia still, and seeing her sad was not something I appreciated.

"Yes, babes. Let's meet up, of course. You're in Florida, right? Meet me at the Chinese restaurant next to Weiss Memorial," I said, and we hung up. I got dressed again, and I rushed to get to her. Olivia had always had my back when we were still in contact. And I wanted to be there for her as well. When I reached the restaurant, she was already there. I spotted her sitting with some luggage next to the table. I frowned. Her eyes looked puffy, and her hair was messed up. And this was Olivia we were talking about. Olivia was one of the most glamorous persons I knew. Her hair was always done, her nails and makeup as well. So to see her looking so haggard, meant something was actually wrong. I walked to her briskly and sat at her table.

"Babes?" I said. She lifted her head and broke into a smile. She was still very beautiful, that was for sure.

"Kelly. You came," Olivia said, and I smiled.

"Of course, I came Oli. You said you needed my help," I replied.

"I don't know... I thought since we hadn't spoken to each other in so long, you would actually come. Thank you Kels," she said, and I nodded.

"Have you ordered anything? Or maybe you should come home instead and get a to-go box?" I suggested, and she nodded gratefully. After we had gotten our food which wasn't long after because the restaurant was virtually empty, we went to my car. We put in the luggage, and I started the car.

"So I'm not going to ask you any questions now because you look really tired. But when we reach, you will take a shower– because you look like shit–, eat, rest, and then we'll talk," I said. Olivia laughed a little. It was an encouraging sound, and I felt happy that I had caused it.

"Deal," she said. The ride home was silent. I knew she was thinking hard because every time I stole a look at her, she had a sad, faraway look on her face. I wanted to hug her.

We reached home, and I showed her where to keep everything. We sat in the living room and started eating. I wanted to ask her about her Daddy, but I had a feeling that everything that was happening right now was because of him. So I kept my mouth shut and just watched her. I guess she was going to talk when she was ready.

"How have you been, Kels?" Olivia asked, and I sighed of happiness.

"And Alex? How is he? Where is he actually?" She asked. I had never told her what he had really been doing to me or how we really was behind closed doors. It wasn't that I didn't feel I could trust her, it was that I wasn't sure how to tell her all the things he had been doing to me without sounding pathetic and even more humiliated. I tensed up at that name. It brought up too many bad memories. And it reminded me of too many things. I cleared my throat.

"Well, Alex is no longer my Daddy," I said, looking away.

"What happened?" she asked with a sympathetic tilt to her head. I sighed.

"A lot of things. But it all comes to the fact that he was abusive, and he cheated on me. Multiple times and in front of me," I explained. I hated going into detail, but I felt she had to know, I guess. Her Daddy and Alex used to be friends.

"Your Daddy didn't tell you all this?" I asked.

"Please don't call him my Daddy. His name is Mike," she said with an angry look on her face. I frowned. So I was right. Mike had indeed caused her a world of pain.

"Oh, sorry. What happened?" I asked.

"If you don't want to talk about it, it's okay." I didn't want her to force herself to do something that she was later on going to regret. I wanted her to be ready when she told me anything.

"No, don't worry about it. It's actually because of that that I am here right now," she said, and I frowned. But I didn't interrupt.

"Mike and I were happy. You know we moved to California and all that. I honestly thought we would be together for a long while. I was thinking long term. Maybe even marriage," she explained, and I nodded. I knew just how committed those two were to each other.

"We saved up. Made a down payment on

the house. But sweetie, what he didn't tell me was he made it in his name only. And every time I asked him, he told me not to worry about it. That it was Daddy stuff." I frowned. That was exactly what Alex used to tell me as well, and we all know how that ended.

"Then a few days ago, he tells me he's getting married," Olivia continued. My mouth dropped.

"What?" I exclaimed.

"Yes. He said he was getting married. And that this lifestyle was just experimentation. That's what he told me. He said he wasn't ready to take care of someone his whole life. He basically said a bunch of stuff that I'm not even ready to repeat yet," she said and laughed sadly. I wanted to hold her, but I refrained myself. I knew from experience that it was just best to let her finish first. Besides, I didn't want her to start crying before she even got to finish the story.

"Kelly, I honestly don't know how I survived that. I didn't even cry in front of him. I don't know how I did it, but I didn't break down, not even once. I stood there, stonily and listened to all his bullshit." I felt so proud of her. Crying in front of people who didn't even care about you was just letting them in on your weaknesses. It never ever worked in your favor. It was just you showing them how desperate you are.

"Then I talked about the house. And I basically asked him what we were going to do about it. Guess what Kels? He had never even put my name on the title. So all my savings, all my efforts were for nothing. He just used me, Kels. He used me, and I hate him for that." That was when the dam burst. Olivia started sobbing. I moved towards her and took her into my arms. I didn't even know what to say. Losing the person you thought loved you then losing all your savings as well. Damn. I didn't even want to imagine how she felt in that moment.

"I couldn't stay there anymore, Kelly. I couldn't stay in that godforsaken town. Then I'd have to look at his face every day, he and his stupid beautiful wife, entering the house that I used my savings to pay for. I just couldn't. I had nowhere else to go. No other friend. I'm sorry for just barging into your life," Olivia said as she started to cry.

"Hey, babes. It's okay. Don't cry. I'm here for you. You're my friend, and I love you. You can count on me any time. Okay?" I said, and she nodded. We just sat there for some time, me hugging her until her tears subsided.

"Thank you so much, Kels. It means a lot." As I was looking at her sad face, the best idea I think I had ever had came into my head.

"Wait. Why don't you just move in with me? We understand each other better than most people do. And we get along well. So as you're getting on your feet, move in with me?"

"Do you really mean this?" Olivia asked. The surprise was evident on her face.

"Yes, babes. Move-in. I love you. And I want to support you in any way I can," I said, and she started sobbing again

"Thank you so much, Kelly. You are such an amazing friend. I don't know what I would have done without you," Olivia said.

***

About thirty minutes later, we had called Thea over because she had complained about not spending enough time with me, and the "squad" was complete. Even though Thea didn't participate in the lifestyle, she was still cool with us talking about it around her.

"So tell us about your Daddy," Olivia said. We were sitting in the bedroom, watching a movie. Even though I'm pretty sure none of us had a clue on what it was about.

"My Daddy is the best in world. I honestly love him so much. Okay, you might feel that I'm too hasty. But he's so good to me. He makes a conscious effort to be what I need, and he tries his best to give me what I need. I really love him," I said dreamily. Both of them were quiet. I looked at them and raised my brows.

"What?" I asked, looking from Olivia to Thea and back to Olivia.

"It's just. I've never see you this way. Not even with Alex," Thea said, looking hesitantly at Olivia, who nodded. I blushed.

"Maybe I feel more? I don't know. But James is good to me," I stated with a bright smile

"We're happy for you, babes. And I hope this lasts. If he hurts you, I don't care if he's 7ft15. I'll hunt him down and rip his balls." This was said by Thea, who was the shortest human being on Earth at 5'1. As we rolled around the floor laughing, I felt a glow of happiness in my heart that I had not felt in years. Then Olivia spoke up.

"I'm happy for you love. You deserve this happiness and more. You are a wonderful person," Olivia said. I wiped the tear that was threatening to fall, and I dragged both of them into a group hug. I couldn't ask for better friends.

Chapter 8

James was supposed to come today. I knew that I wasn't supposed to take any major decisions without him. But last night, when Olivia had cried in front of me, I honestly felt like I had no other choice. She was my friend, and I wanted to support her in every way.

"So have you thought about what you're going to tell your Daddy?" she asked, and I sighed, then shook my head.

"I don't know. I'll just explain what happened to him and he'll understand. He's a great Daddy," I said and smiled.

"He sure does sound like one," Olivia said, and I couldn't help but notice that her tone sounded wistful.

"Don't worry, babes. You'll find a Daddy who will love you the way you're supposed to be love. And he'll see to all your needs," I said, emphasizing the word all. I hugged her, and she leaned into me.

"I'll go the bedroom for a bit," she said, then she walked to the room. I watched her walk away and sighed. Olivia was such a beautiful person. She deserved way more than all she was getting. At that moment, Daddy came in. My eyes widened.

"Daddy! You're here early," I exclaimed, standing from the couch and going into his arms.

"Yes Princess. You didn't want me to come?" Daddy teased, and I laughed.

"Of course, I did. I missed you so much yesterday. I thought you were ignoring me," I confessed, putting my head down. He carried me to the couch and sat me in his lap

"And how could I ever ignore you? You're my princess. I always try my best to make time for you," he said and placed a kiss on my lips. "So what did you do yesterday? And what's that?" he asked, looking at the ashtray. I widened my eyes. I had forgotten entirely that Olivia smoked. And she had left her ashtray in the living room. I was going to kill that girl.

"I.. uh, it's mine?" I said or more like asked.

"I know you don't smoke. What are you hiding from me, Kelly?" Daddy asked, and I bit my lip.

"Nothing, Daddy," I said, pushing him onto the couch.

"Are you lying to me right now?" Daddy asked with narrowed eyes and a tone that said I'd better tell him the truth. I sighed and nodded.

"What was rule number 4?" James asked, looking at me with a smirk.

"Never lie to Daddy," I said with a pout. I hated that I couldn't get away with anything.

"And what did you just do?" James questioned, reaching out and tucking my hair behind my ears.

"I lied Daddy," I said, looking down at my feet.

"Now you'll tell me what exactly you lied to me about. Starting from whose ashtray that is," James demanded. When Daddy got like this, I knew not to mess with him, so I hurried to tell him what had happened.

"Well, Daddy, I have a friend over. She came in yesterday. And she didn't have anywhere else to go. So I told her to move in. Wait! Daddy! Before you say anything, I know I should have told you about it. But she's really stranded, and her Daddy left her. I just felt so sad," I trailed out and lay my head on his shoulder.

"Go get your friend," Daddy ordered as he pushed me gently off his lap. I walked to the room and saw Olivia sitting on the bed. I knew from the expression her face that she had been listening to everything

"I hope I didn't get you into trouble?" she asked with a worried expression on her face.

"No, don't worry about it. He'll probably punish me, and that'll be all about it," I explained and held her hand. We walked to the living room, and Daddy was standing with his back to us.

"Daddy," I called, and he turned.

"Hi," Olivia said, waving. I could tell that

Daddy was impressed by Olivia's features. We were the same height, but our appearances were very different. Olivia was a blonde with startlingly clear green eyes. She had the most beautiful features that beckoned you to her. I hadn't met someone yet that wasn't impressed with her. She was a very beautiful woman.

"And who might you be?" Daddy asked as he approached us.

"I'm Olivia. Kelly's friend. Please don't punish her! She didn't do anything. She was just being a good friend to me," Olivia said, and I held my breath waiting for Daddy's reaction

"So she told you I was going to punish her, huh?" Olivia didn't answer, just bit her lip. I sighed. He was probably going to up the punishment now.

"What we are going to do is, I'll give Kelly's punishment, and you, Olivia, will watch. Is that clear?" Daddy asked, and I let out a sigh of relief. I knew he would never push my limits, but sometimes I got inexplicably scared. I nodded, and Olivia took that as her cue to nod as well.

"Come to the bedroom now," he said, and we followed him dutifully. Daddy sat at the edge of the bed, motioned for Olivia to sit opposite him. He gave me a look, and I already knew what it meant. I climbed into his lap and took in a deep breath as he removed my clothes. I wasn't scared he was going to hurt me. I was just nervous because it was the first time that I was getting punished in front of someone else. I swallowed as he repeated what he always did.

"Count out after each spank. If not, I'll start all over again. I'll give you ten spanks," he said, and I nodded, even though he didn't technically needed me to agree. The first spank was a surprise. But for some reason, my pussy clenched on nothing, already getting moist.

"One," I shouted. The next one was even more arousing.

"You're getting wet. You like that, huh?" Daddy said, then he placed a light spank on my pussy. I gasped spread my legs even more. After five spanks, I turned to look at Olivia, and I almost smiled. She had that look on her face. I knew she was turned on. I had seen her turned on before when we had had scenes at the kink club. And with the way she kept on changing her positions in the chair. Our eyes met, and I winked at her. She blushed.

"Look how wet your pussy is," Daddy said when he was done spanking me.

"Do you want me to touch you? To finger you until you come?" James teased.

"Yes, please, Daddy," I whined, gyrating my ass in his lap. He slapped my ass lightly then he asked a question that made me pause a little.

"Do you think I should let her cum Olivia?" James asked.

"Um, yes, sir," Olivia replied. I could tell from Olivia's voice that she was just as shocked. Daddy slapped my ass again, then traced the outline of my wetness lightly with his finger. I clenched it and whined a little. Then finally, he inserted the finger to the hilt and fucked it slowly.

"More, please, Daddy," I said. Daddy added

another finger, then another, and started thrusting fast. I held his wrist and started riding his fingers, moaning out. At this point, I didn't even care if Olivia was in the room or not. I just wanted to cum.

"Yes, Daddy," I screamed as the orgasm hit me. Then I let go of his hand and slumped in his lap.

***

After a bath, Daddy changed both Olivia and I. We were both wearing onesies, hers was purple, and mine was pink. We were sitting in the living room when he brought out a mat and placed a couple of toys on it. There was something about seeing all my toys in one place that made me regress. I couldn't even explain it. Once I had my pacifier in my mouth, my diaper and onesie on, and my toys placed out, I just couldn't help it. Apparently it was the same for Olivia. Daddy was watching us play with a smile on his face.

"Want to have a team party?" I asked Olivia.

My age space was between 8 to 10, but I think Olivia was younger. Because she couldn't even articulate properly.

"Tea Party!" she exclaimed, and I smiled.

"Daddy, can we have a tea party?" I asked Daddy, turning towards him.

"Sure, Princess. Where's your tea set?" he asked, and I pointed with a tilt to my head.

"Even when you regress, you're bossy," Daddy muttered playfully, but I still heard him. I laughed a little. He brought the tea set. I helped Olivia, who was still playing with her stuffies, to sit properly. I put a cup in front of her. Then I looked up at Daddy.

"Daddy, won't you join us?" I asked, giving him my infamous puppy eyes.

"Sure, Princess," he said, then came and sat in one of the chairs. I laughed a little at how ridiculous he looked, but I placed a cup in front of me. I poured the tea into their cups. I laughed when instead of drinking, Olivia took the cup and started hitting it against the table. I looked over at

Daddy, who was staring at me already. I blushed, and a feeling of contentment came over me. Then I let out a loud gasp as a great idea came to my head.

"Daddy, why don't you be Olivia's Daddy too?" I asked.

Chapter 9

Today we were heading over to Daddy's house. After the last time, after I had blurted my question, he had scolded me a little. But I knew it was something he wanted as well. So I pushed for it. So when Olivia came out of her regression, I brought it up again. Innocently. Not at all subtly. I just went, "Olivia don't you want my Daddy to be your Daddy as well?" I think she thought I was testing her cause she grew flustered and shook her headfirst. But I knew she was lying. Daddy, too, was lying. They both wanted to be in each other's lives, but they were scared of my reaction. I honestly was okay with it. Olivia was one of my closest friends, and I loved her a lot. And James was my Daddy. I loved him too. And honestly, I didn't mind if we shared this love we had for each other together. Neither of them had agreed, but I was still going to try and convince them because I thought they just needed a little push. So I had convinced Olivia to come with me to Daddy's house.

We reached Daddy's place in record time. When we got in, Daddy was in the living room. He wasn't even surprised to see Olivia with me. He said, "Good. You brought Olivia along," and it left me wondering what exactly he meant by that. But I didn't press and just watched him. He told us both to sit. I looked Olivia to make sure she was comfortable. I definitely didn't want to drag her into something that she felt weird about. I didn't want to be that friend.

"So I thought about what you said yesterday a lot, Kelly," Daddy started, and I had to curb my victorious smile. I knew that Daddy had been thinking about it. I knew my Daddy.

"And while it is true that Olivia and I don't know much about each other yet, I would love to be her Daddy. Olivia, is this something you would be interested in?" Daddy asked. I felt like squealing. This was the most awesome thing ever.

I looked over at Olivia as both Daddy and I waited for a response from her.

"Yes," she said quietly. I knew Daddy didn't like that. He liked it when you speak up loudly and clearly.

"What was that? Speak clearly. And you can call me Daddy if you agree," Daddy added.

"Yes, Daddy," was Olivia's response, and I couldn't help it. I squealed this time around. I jumped from where I was sitting and ran to Daddy and hugged him. Then I placed a kiss on his mouth.

"You're the best Daddy ever, in the whole wide world," I said and kissed him again. He laughed, then held me. Both of us turned out glances towards Olivia, who was still sitting there.

"Come here, little one," Daddy said to Olivia lovingly. Olivia reacted instantly. She ran towards him as well and jumped into his arms. He placed both of us on both his laps.

"Okay, now. I have a surprise for both of y'all. I'll need you to stay patient. I don't want any show of impatience. If not, I'll punish you. Okay?"

James instructed, looking more at me than Olivia. I knew I had a way of being impatient, but he didn't need to rub it in.

"Yes, Daddy," we chorused.

"Good," come James's short answer as he set us down on the couch, then went and picked something up from the table. They were blindfolded. He tied both our eyes, starting with Olivia.

"I'll carry both of you to the bedroom. And when I place you on the floor, you're to stay in the same spot. Don't move, okay?" James instructed. I loved it when he did things like this.

"Yes, Daddy," we chorused again. I felt Daddy's arms against my back as he lifted me into his powerful arms. I giggled a little, and Daddy placed a kiss on my forehead. We reached the bedroom, and he set me on a soft and comfortable surface.

"If you peek, I'll know," was all Daddy said before he left the room. I waited for him to come along with Olivia. The urge to just lift the blindfold and peek was extremely strong. But I controlled myself and say dutifully like a good girl. I didn't want to spoil the surprise for all three of us. I heard Daddy's footsteps, and I perked up. After a few rustles, he said, "Okay, now you can lift your blindfolds." I lifted my blindfold slowly, and I was in awe at what I saw. It was an actual nursery. Not just a play spot with a couple of toys. A nursery. I looked at Olivia, and I could tell that she was just as awed as me. The theme of the room was baby pink, which was my favorite color and I think Olivia's as well. There were two cribs in the room and in the cribs were a bunch of stuffies. There was a huge section filled with just toys, and I couldn't wait to play there. Then there was a tea table. There were also video games and a console for us to play.

"I hope you like it." Daddy's voice brought me out of my awestruck state. I looked at him like he was mad.

"Like it? Daddy, we love it. Right, Olivia?" I asked since she wasn't saying anything. She smiled at me, then turned to Daddy and said, "We do. Thank you, Daddy."

"Thank you, Daddy," I repeated. I stood from wherever Daddy had placed me which was a bean bag by the way and ran to him.

"I love you so much, Daddy. Can we explore?" I asked, clapping my hand.

"Go right ahead, princess. It's your nursery," was Daddy's response. This man really wanted me to love him even more than I did right now. I walked around, touching everything with awe. Alex had never offered me this, not even when we were okay. It was all so new to me, but I loved going around the room and touching everything I could get my hands on.

"When you are done, tell me. We need to go over some things," Daddy said, then left the room.

"Are you sure you really don't mind sharing your Daddy?" Olivia asked as soon as Daddy left the room.

"I wouldn't have proposed if I minded, right? I love you. I really do. And I want your happiness. I feel that we will be very happy together, all three of us," I explained, and she nodded.

"I love you, Kels," Olivia said, then she pulled me into a long hug.

"Let's go find Daddy," I said, grabbing her hand and running through the house. We smiled at each other then I led her to Daddy's bedroom. I knew he was probably going to be in there. And I was right. He was sitting on the bed, and he looked up when we came in.

"Hi Daddy," I said, and he motioned for us to walk to him. When we reached, he placed each of us on either side of his lap. Then he showed the papers he had been looking at. It was my contract. I felt kind of possessive when I saw it, which was kind of stupid. Why didn't I feel possessive over Daddy? Just over the contract? I sighed and decided not to mull over it more than necessary. It was of no use trying to understand my thoughts sometimes. So I listened to whatever Daddy was saying.

"So I set up more rules. Kelly already knows them. But you don't know them, Olivia. So we'll leave you some time to read. You read them and tell me if you don't understand anything, alright?" James asked, patting my bottom lovingly.

"Yes, Daddy," she replied and started reading. I leaned in Daddy's shoulder and watched her for a while. Then I got bored. I started playing with the collar of Daddy's shirt, and he hugged me close to him.

"Are you sure you're okay with this? I know you're the one who proposed it in the first place, but I want to know that you're completely okay before we proceed to anything," Daddy said, and my heart warmed at his thoughtfulness.

"Yes, Daddy. I love both of you. And I feel we need each other. I don't know why," I explained so he could understand my motives more.

"Olivia's Daddy left her in a really bad state, and she needs love. She's a bit like me, Daddy. She needs you. She needs us," I explained. Daddy looked at me for a while without saying a word.

Then he kissed me on the forehead.

"You're a gem. I love you," James said, kissing the top of my head. Soon enough, Olivia was done reading.

"Done?" Daddy asked, and she nodded.

"Is there anything you're not comfortable with?" James asked.

"Uh, yes, Daddy. The smoking rule..." She started, but Daddy interrupted her.

"We will start off slowly, but I want you to drop it. I know you are addicted to it. But for now, we'll go progressively. Okay?" Daddy asked, and Olivia nodded.

"Thank you, Daddy," she said shyly then placed a kiss on his cheek. I was happy.

***

The next day was beautiful. I had never felt that way before. Olivia and I slept with Daddy, and it was honestly one of the best feelings in my life. We were up for the day now and sitting in the dining table, waiting for Daddy to serve us breakfast. Since we were two of us, I doubted that he was going to feed us both. I didn't mind, though. It was going to be tiring if he tried something like that. As he placed the food in front of us, we both said thanks. Then dug in. As soon as Olivia took a bite of her food, though, she said, "Fuck!" I looked up at her then looked at Daddy. He hadn't heard. Because he wasn't looking at us. And he hadn't turned to scold Olivia or anything.

"You need to tell Daddy," I said, looking up at her worriedly. I didn't want to tell on her. But not telling Daddy was going to be breaking two rules. Olivia bit her lip and said, "I know. Let's finish eating." I nodded. At that moment, I started imagining the punishment scene, and I started feeling left out. But I didn't want to be a bad girl either. I didn't want to do something and just to purposely get a spanking from Daddy. So I refrained myself. As Daddy was clearing the plates, Olivia said, "Daddy, I... I broke a rule. I'm sorry, Daddy. I said a bad word." Her lip was trembling as he looked up at Daddy. He packed up the plates, placed them in the sink, then walked back to us.

"Come. Let's go for your punishment. And baby girl, come along. You're going to watch," he told me, and I stood eagerly. We went to the bedroom.

"I'll give you five spanks, Olivia. Because you told me right away. Come here," Daddy said. Olivia went to him. I watched as he undressed her and put her in his lap. For the first time since I had said Olivia and I should share Daddy, I felt jealous. There was some connection that I couldn't explain in spanking. And seeing Olivia taking advantage of it and not me saddened me. Daddy noticed. "What's wrong, Princess?" he asked, and I sighed a little.

"Can I have a spanking, too, Daddy?" I asked.

"Did you do anything wrong?" Daddy asked, and I shook my head.

"Then why do you want a spanking?" James asked.

"It makes me feel closer to you," I confessed. Daddy looked at me for a while then beckoned me to him.

"We'll give you three spanks. Count each of them out," he said, then placed me in his lap. I felt fulfilled. Or maybe it wasn't the right word. I just couldn't explain it. Having my Daddy discipline me was something I would always be thankful for and never get tired of.

Chapter 10

It was weekend again, which was the only time Olivia and I could spend time without Daddy. This was because Olivia had found a job. She was working as a secretary at a publishing company. I had my shifts at the hospital, and Daddy did too. Friday, Daddy had picked us up and drove over to his place. We had all missed each other because as soon as Olivia and I saw him, we launched at him with hugs. Hugs he received with just as much affection. I loved just how affectionate Daddy was. He always made sure to give us hugs, kisses, and show us generally that he loved and appreciated us. It wasn't even about sex. I could count the number of times we had had sex. He was just a really awesome Daddy. It was Daddy who woke both of us up the next morning.

"I've run a bath for you. Come to the bathroom," he said. We had ignored our cribs again and slept with him in his bedroom. In my opinion, it was way better. I loved knowing the fact that my two favorite people were sleeping next to me, and I could reach out and touch them any time. Olivia and I stripped and followed Daddy to the bathroom. I think I squealed a little when I got to the bath. The water was pink! And there were lots of toys floating on it. It was so pretty.

"It's so pretty, Daddy!" Olivia exclaimed, stealing the thoughts right out of my mouth. I nodded, and daddy smiled. I loved it when Daddy smiled.

"You look so handsome when you smile, Daddy," I said, smiling at him. I swear a blush appeared on Daddy's skin! Daddy was blushing!

"Thank you, princess," he said.

"You're all red, Daddy," I teased, and we laughed.

"Get into that bath, little brat," James said, making me giggle. I got into the bath after sticking my tongue at Daddy. Both Olivia and I were in the tub, and I splashed water at her. She laughed, and she retaliated, making both of us giggle.

"Bubbles," Olivia whispered in awe when we splashed the water a little too much and bubbles form. I picked one up and poked at it curiously, then giggle when it bursts. Then I took another and opened my mouth. As I was about to put it on my tongue, Olivia burst it, and we giggled.

"Don't put it anywhere near your mouths," Daddy warned, and we nodded. We kept playing. Then Daddy stopped us. He washed me first, then got me out of the water with instructions to towel myself dry. I used the towel and wiped off all the water I could and watched Daddy as he washed Olivia in the bath. I almost want to go join them again, but Daddy carried Olivia out if the bathtub and ordered her to towel herself dry as well. I watched with fascination as Daddy pulled out the plug, and the water started draining out of the bathtub. And don't ask why I found it fascinating. It just was. We followed Daddy to the room. I sat on the beanbag watching as Daddy changed Olivia. He put her diaper on, took a cute blue onesie, and made her wear it. Then he put the paci in her mouth. Then it was my turn. It was always so comforting how Daddy took care of me. It was in the little things. How he gave us baths, dressed us, fed us and was just there overall for him. I wanted to be there for him as well. I hoped he was happy.

"Daddy, are you happy with us?" I asked, looking at him intently. I knew Daddy well enough by now to know when he was lying or hurt.

"I am princess. You brighten up my world," Daddy said, then he placed a kiss on my lips. I smiled, satisfied. He wasn't lying. He really was happy with us. And I was happy about that. I wouldn't want to be in a relationship where just one party was happy. It was interesting, hurtful, and draining. When we were both dressed, we went to the part of the nursery that doubled as a playpen. I didn't really want to play, so I watched as Olivia played with her stuffies.

"Is anything wrong, baby?" Daddy asked, and I sighed.

"No, Daddy. I just... my princess parts are

tingling," I said in a small voice.

"And you want me to take care of it?" Daddy asked, and I nodded. We went to Daddy's room alongside Olivia. I was excited. This was the first time that I was initiating things, especially now that Olivia was here. And I didn't know how everything was going to go. But I was so excited. As soon as we reached the bedroom, Daddy ordered both of us to take off our clothes. When we did so, he took off our diapers. None of us was wet and messy, so he kissed us and told us we were good girls.

"Both of you, lay in bed," Daddy ordered. We scrambled to obey, and we both did lay, watching him walk around the room. I wanted to know what he was going to tell me to do next.

"Are your princess parts still tingling Kelly?" Daddy asked.

"Yes, Daddy," I responded, hoping that he was going to do something about it.

"What about yours, Olivia?" he continued, and I risked a glance at Olivia. I didn't know she felt this way too.

"Yes, Daddy," she answers as well.

"Touch yourselves. I want you to spread those pink pussy lips for Daddy, spread them, and touch your hard little clits." I swallowed at the feeling that Daddy's words were giving me, and I followed his instructions. I spread my lower lips and placed a finger on my clit. I rubbed it and let out a low moan, writhing a little when the pleasure increased.

"Now what you're going to do is Olivia, get down. Spread Kelly's lips, and suck on her clit." I watched Olivia as she did what Daddy told her to do. Her soft hands on my lips were such a turn on, and when she took my clit into her mouth, I almost lost it. I closed my eyes and let out a loud moan. This was one of the best feelings in the world.

"Liv..." I moaned out, closing my eyes and threading my fingers through her hair.

"That's enough. Olivia lay back. Kelly do the same thing." It was such a turn on to be hearing Daddy's orders. I spread Olivia's legs a little, then touched her pussy lightly with my index finger. I opened up her lips and rubbed the clit a little, enjoying how she writhed in pleasure. There was a lot of juice coming from her hole. I bent and took her clit into my mouth, making sure to suck on it.

"Oh yes, Kels. Oh my God, that feels so good," she said, and I preened at the praise.

"That's enough now," Daddy said, and I reluctantly removed my mouth from Olivia's pussy.

"Now, you'll kiss and taste each other." I advanced towards Olivia and placed my hand on her beautiful face. I leaned in for a kiss, and our lips met. Her lips were soft to the touch, and I knew I was going to enjoy this. I deepened the kiss, and I could feel my juices flowing even more as her sweet tongue explored my mouth.

"That's enough," Daddy said, and when we looked at him, he was naked. His hand was stroking his big erection. Then he climbed on the bed as well and lay down.

"Kelly, climb on my cock and ride it. Olivia,

come sit on my face," James ordered. I went eagerly. I wanted to shock daddy and please him even more, so before sitting on his cock, I put it in my mouth and sucked on it a little. I knew he liked that by the little groan he released. Then I let go of it with a pop. I straddled his laps and guided his erection into my very wet hole. When he slid to the hilt, I let out a loud moan. I hadn't felt this in so long, and it felt like heaven.

"Don't ride yet," Daddy commanded, and I tried my best to curb my desires. I watched as Olivia straddled Daddy's face, facing me. Then I felt Daddy jerk his hips up, a signal that I could start riding. I placed my hands on both sides of his legs and started riding slowly, enjoying the feeling of his dick against my walls. It was the best feeling in the world. I looked up and saw Olivia, who was also riding his face. I leaned forward and kissed her, enhancing the whole experience even more. Then I let go and let out a huge gasp. It was almost like Daddy had gotten bigger in me. I started riding him even quicker, not minding the sweat that was dripping from my boobs. The pleasure was only intensifying, and I felt like I was going to pass out at any moment from it.

"Oh my God, Daddy," I heard Olivia scream, and I think it sparked my own orgasm. Because at that moment, the waves of pleasure hit me. I kept riding them and screaming, my eyes closed, and my back arched. I continued riding Daddy until he jerked powerfully one last time and put his cum in me. Olivia got down from Daddy's face, and I leaned forward and kissed him. Then kissed her.

"I love you, Daddy. I love you, Olivia," I said as happy tears welled up in my eyes. This was honestly one of the best experiences of my entire life.

Chapter 11

It had been a month since Olivia had come into our lives, and everything was going smoothly. Since all three of us had had sex, it had become a regular thing. Sometimes, Daddy would tell us to each other out. Or one of us would eat the other out while the latter sucked on his cock. It was different from all the experiences I had had before, and I wasn't complaining. Matter of fact, it was something I really enjoyed. After the initial possessiveness, I had felt every time Daddy had to punish Olivia, which wasn't often cause she was a really good girl, everything else had gone really smoothly. It was funny how Alex used to bring littles in front of me to taunt me, and I got jealous. But here I was, sharing a Daddy with one of my closest friends and feeling good about the whole thing. It wasn't that I loved Daddy less. It definitely wasn't the case. Or that I considered Olivia inferior to me or something. That was not it either. I loved my Daddy very much. And I believed without being biased that Olivia was one of the most beautiful people that graced the earth. The thing is I knew and trusted both of them. And maybe my trust was going to backfire, but I didn't think so. I believed all three of us loved each other. And if I was being honest, I had started loving Olivia, more than just a friend. I had just gotten back from work. I got into the house and frowned a little. The house was messy. And with two people like Olivia and I living in it, this house was never messy. We were extremely neat and made sure to keep everything where it was supposed to be, so I didn't understand. Nevertheless, I walked to the bedroom, and I saw that it was even messier than the living room. I frowned.

"Olivia?" I called, wondering where she was.

"In here!" The voice was coming from the bathroom, so I walked there and opened the door. This room was no exception. It was almost like a hurricane had come and swept through the room, leaving only one side of the stuff on my side untouched.

"What's happening? Why is everything so messy?" I asked, watching her weigh two bottles before throwing them both into a bag.

"And what are you packing?" I questioned, biting my bottom lip.

"I'm so sorry, Kels. I meant to be gone before you came. But I guess since you're here, oh well."

"Where are you moving to?" I asked, a strange feeling coming over me. I didn't like where this was going. And I honestly wasn't sure that I was going to like her answer.

"James didn't tell you? I'm moving in with him," Olivia announced brightly, and I tilted my head to the side. I probably had misunderstood because Olivia didn't just say that she was moving in with my Daddy.

"What did you say? You're moving in with who?" I asked again. I wasn't the type of get into flights. But I would honestly fight her if she thought she was going to do me dirty like this. Then I was going to meet that bullhead of James and punch him in the face, no matter how hard it hurt my hand.

"I said, I'm moving in with James, and I. The both of us, we reached the conclusion that I will be his little. Exclusively. I love you, and I'm really sorry Kelly. I honestly didn't mean for any of this to happen," Olivia explained. My resolve weakened. I didn't even know what to do at this point. The tears filled my eyes, and I turned away before an ugly sob left my chest. This was what I was dreading. Why did everyone leave me? Why? Was I some kind of monster?

"Oh my God, Kels. Please don't cry," Olivia said, and I felt like slapping her at that moment.

"Olivia, if you really don't want to go meet your Daddy"– I sneered the word– "with a black eye, then you'll refrain from speaking to me," I growled.

"Kels, please, I was just kidding. I wanted

this to be a surprise. James asked both of us to move in with him. You know I love you too much to do something like that to you. Please forgive me. I admit it was a joke in bad taste," Olivia said, realizing the pain she had just caused me. When I heard those words, I turned to Olivia with a murderous expression of my face.

"I've never been so scared before in my life. Please don't repeat that," I said coldly then walked out of the room. I went to the bedroom, cried a little then went back to the bathroom. Olivia was sitting there with a dejected look on her face. I sighed when I saw her.

"You're forgiven. Stop looking like a puppy that was run over," I said, rolling my eyes. Olivia woke up suddenly and launched herself at me.

"Thank you, Kels. I don't know what I was thinking with your past and all. I was just trying to be... I just wanted to play a prank on you," she explained, and she looked so sad that I rolled my eyes and hugged her.

"It's okay. Just don't repeat it," I said, and

she nodded frantically. Then she placed a small kiss on my lips and walked away. I took another bag and joined her to start packing.

"When did James have the time to tell you all this?" I was curious because I knew that he got out of work even later than me sometimes.

"He came home and met me. He told me he was going to finalize some things. I don't know what, though," she said, and I let out a small mhmm. I continued packing. Then we moved to the living room. Looking at everything was overwhelming. Daddy's house was already completely furnished, so I didn't know what we were going to do with all this. Unless we like rented a storage unit and the rent of those things didn't come for cheap.

"Daddy said we should leave everything else. He'd take care of it," Olivia supplied helpfully when she saw me looking at everything.

"Oh, okay," I said. I left. I was feeling kinda jealous at that moment. But I knew that once I had decided to share, I had taken the consequences as well. I couldn't leave the relationship though because of some petty jealousy. I was just going to spend five to ten minutes alone to clear my head. It always worked. And it did this time. I got out of the bedroom, where I had been moping a little. Olivia was standing there, a worried look on her face.

"Are you okay?" she asked.

"Yes, babes. I'm sorry sometimes I just have to remind myself that neither of you is going to betray me. I get in my feelings sometimes. I'm sorry," I said with a sigh.

"Hey, no need to apologize. Honestly, you're very strong. You welcomed me into your home, and you welcomed me into your Daddy's arms. I love just how strong you are because, to be honest with you. I'm not sure that I would have done same. I am so proud of you," Olivia explained. I teared up and took Olivia into my arms. We stayed there for quite a long time. That was how Daddy found us.

"My two princesses," he said, and we let go of each other. Both of us jumped and ran towards him.

"Daddy I missed you so much," I said as he hugged us right to him.

"I missed you too little one," Daddy said, and I smiled.

"Are you done packing?" be asked, and both of us hopelessly shook our heads.

"Have you packed the essentials, though?" he asked.

"Yes, Daddy," Olivia answered since I had barely had time to pack anything.

"Good. I will get the bags, and we will finish packing all this tomorrow. Because I guess we're all tired."

"Okay, Daddy. Thank you, Daddy. You're the best Daddy ever," I said and kissed his cheek. We showed Daddy where the bags were, and he took them out to his car. Then buckled us into the car, and we drove off to his place. It was a quick ride as there wasn't a lot of traffic.

"Welcome home, princess. Welcome home, cupcake," Daddy said as soon as we got into the house.

***

It was time to lay down everything. We were sitting in the living room, Olivia and I next to each other. We were waiting for Daddy to say something.

"Okay, so I have destroyed the other contract. Both of you will read this one and if you are displeased with anything. If you're not, though, you can sign right away," James said. He gave both of us the contracts. The title was OUR DDLG RELATIONSHIP: JAMES, KELLY, AND OLIVIA. I liked my name was first. I started reading through and nodding my head as I agreed with everything that James had written. He had asked us what type of things we would like in the contract before he wrote it up, I liked that he did stuff like that. The only thing that had my concerned was the fact that Daddy had added one rule about smoking. I was worried that Olivia would not be able to quit just because he told her to. I asked Daddy for a pen and signed. A while after, Olivia signed as well. When she did, we looked at each other and squealed. Then we hugged each other. We were officially littles to our Daddy.

Chapter 12

Olivia's POV

Today was great. And it was going to keep being awesome. I had come back from work early. And what James had told me when I got back home had put me in an instant good mood. Firstly, all three of us were going to go out and get dinner. Then we were going to do a scene at the kink club. I didn't know why, but Daddy had said this scene was going to be special, and I believed him. He was my Daddy, after all. We waited for Kelly to get back from work. Honestly, I didn't know what I would have done without her in my life. I would probably be stranded somewhere, lost, alone, and lonely. But because of her, I had a Daddy now. And every day, I was loving her more and more, and not just as a friend. When she came back, I relayed the news to her. Daddy gave us an hour to get ready for dinner. And his exact words were, "Even if you're not ready in an hour, I'm dragging you out, naked or clothed."

An hour wasn't a lot, but we could do something with it. Both of us showered. Then we proceeded to get ready. Yes. We were littles. But that didn't mean that we weren't in touch with our feminity. We started with our hair. While I did big curls, Kelly straightened hers. Then we moved on to makeup. We kept it quite simple, the only extra thing being the lipstick we put on. Then we put our dresses and shoes on, and we were good to go.

We went to a fancy restaurant. It was like Daddy was celebrating something, but he didn't want to let us in on the joke. We were left wondering. And we didn't have a lot of options because right after dinner, we had a scene. I hadn't been in a public scene for about a year now. And I honestly couldn't wait. It was something I enjoyed doing. It made me let go of my inhibitions. And it took all my stress away. I felt so free when I was doing a scene. It was liberating. Soon enough, we were done with dinner. Daddy drove us to the club. We stood around for a while with the other littles. They knew now that we shared a Daddy, and it was good that all of them were open-minded because none of them judged.

"Honestly, if I had the chance to share him with you guys, I would take it," one of our friends said.

"Don't tell my Daddy I said that though," she added sheepishly, and we laughed. From the way they were talking, I knew just how lucky I was to have a friend and lover like Kelly. She was so selfless. She had agreed to share her Daddy with me. And it baffled me every single time that I looked at James. It made me realize just how much I loved her.

"Did Daddy tell you we'll have a scene tonight?" I asked her sipping at the juice in my class. These clothes were restricting. I wanted to be naked or in a diaper. Not in the skintight red dress I had decided to wear. I noticed Kelly fidgeting as well, and I concluded that she had the same problem.

"Yes, and he made it sound so ominous. Maybe it's because it's his first scene," she said.

"Maybe," was my only reply.

"Go get ready for the scene," Daddy whispered to us. I shivered at his voice and obeyed him. I couldn't wait. I couldn't wait to be completely possessed by him.

James's POV

Handcuffs. I had handcuffed both of them. I felt in control. They couldn't do anything. Black blindfolds. Just enough to keep them from knowing exactly what I wanted to do. I wanted them to anticipate every move I was going to make. Every kiss I was going to place on their bodies. Every touch I was going to trace into their skin. I wanted to keep them from seeing me lick my lips at their beautiful bodies and seductive postures. I didn't want them to see me walk towards them. But I didn't want their senses numb. I wanted them to feel my presence behind them. I wanted them to feel my breath as I traced it across their earlobes. I wanted them to shiver when I gently traced their backs with my finger. I wanted them to feel me touch their sides, run my hands along their hips, and trace it right up to their soft breasts, barely touching them. I wanted them to feel me. I wanted them to know just who their Daddy was.

I started by tugging on their shirts. Every movement I made to one, I made to the other. It was dark, but I could tell who was who. I just didn't want to let it matter at this moment. All that counted right now was me touching them and giving them pleasure. I knew that they couldn't take off their shirts alone. And even if they could, their hands were cuffed. So I tugged on the shirt made a hole. I repeated the same process with the next person. Then I tugged at those holes. I pulled until their gorgeous black bra just barely covered the skin on their chests. I kissed their necks, making sure to alternate and whisper some exciting thing into their ears. Then I moved my lips up to their mouths and kissed them, one after the other, passionately. Their moans made me almost lose control. I wanted much more.

Oh, God. Did I want more? I wanted so much more of them than there was revealed. They looked so sexy there. Vulnerable. The excitement in their bodies. From their quivering thighs to their shaky breaths. They were scared. Not scared of me. They were scared of the unknown. But it was obvious that they wanted this. They wanted more. Their little moans and tight nipples gave them away. They didn't know what I was going to do next. And that made them even more excited. And it made them feel powerful yet so powerless at the same time. Slowly, and teasingly I moved my hand down to their underwear and rubbed at their princess parts. I was standing in the middle, where I could easily touch them both, as much as I wanted to. I knew they weren't ready yet for me to touch their wet, quivering pussy lips. But I did. And I rubbed until I had them moaning. Oh, God, the sound of their moans together. It was like I was listening to the sweetest music.

One of them moaned again before I put my hand inside their panties. I slowly slipped a finger inside her. Felt how bad they were clenching against me. Almost as if they were in sync, both of them moaned very loudly. I alternated kisses on their backs, making them moan even more. I knew that they were close to cumming. Even though I had barely done anything yet.

"Don't cum yet, baby girl," I said, moving my fingers in and out of both of rhythmically. I knew it excited both if them that they didn't know who exactly I was talking to.

"Don't. Not yet." One of them moaned and squirmed around, trying so hard not to.

"You look so sexy, trying not to cum." She moaned as I added another finger and moved faster. I felt her pulse and felt her quiver. Both of them were so close. But I didn't want them to cum yet. I had more interesting things to do to them. I removed my fingers completely, ignoring their moans if protest. One after the other, I removed their panties completely, making sure to drop little slaps on their wet pussies. Then I bent and licked her soaking princess parts, and repeated the same thing with the other.

"Don't you fucking cum yet.." I said quietly.

"Daddy...please..." Kelly whispered. She was more sensitive.

"No." I licked both of them more and more. Tasting their delicious wet parts. I pushed my tongue completely into each of them alternatively, and Olivia screamed.

"You can cum now, baby girl." She sighed, gasped and screamed, and came all over. Then as if in tempo, Kelly let out a loud scream as well and came. I didn't uncuff them. And I didn't remove the blindfolds. I took one of the collars, went to Kelly, put it around her neck and locked it. "I love you, baby girl," I whispered and placed a small kiss on her mouth. I walked the other way to Olivia with the other collar, did the same as I had done for Kelly, then placed a kiss on her lips as well.

"I love you cupcake." After doing that, I removed the blindfolds and handcuffs. The scene was officially over.

Chapter 13

Kelly's POV

Daddy had collared us. He had collared us! The scene was the most beautiful one of my entire existence, and I wasn't sure that anything else could top it. Being collared was serious. It was basically marriage. It was telling us just how serious he was about us. I loved him so much. I didn't know how I could show him. But I loved him so much. Olivia and I went out to get him a gift to show him just how much we loved him. And we also wanted our mark on him. Call it being possessive. We didn't care. No other person was going to look at our man.

"Do you think he'd like this?" Olivia asked, lifting up a bracelet. We were at a jewelry store trying to find something for him, and it was turning out to be kind of a struggle.

"He would never even be able to wear it. He would have to remove it at the hospital," I said, sighing. It was hard buying a gift for a doctor when the job was so practical. Olivia sighed. I sighed again. Then a brilliant idea crossed my mind.

"Why don't we get him a chain. A beautiful silver chain, maybe?" I asked, looking at Olivia for her input. She was smiling.

"That's a great idea. And then we add two rings to it because he's ours. And no one will ever approach him!" she exclaimed, and I laughed.

"That's a great idea," I replied. We started looking for the items. Olivia was looking for the rings while I was looking for the chain. I found something. It was simple, and it honestly screamed James

"Daddy will like it," Olivia said when I showed her. She had gotten two beautiful silver rings. After paying, we left the shop and went back home.

Daddy was already home when we got there,

which was a huge surprise. We looked at each other because normally he was home way later than all this. So we didn't really understand what he was doing home.

"Hi Daddy," I said, placing a kiss on his cheek. Olivia did the same thing, and he smiled at both of us. I loved seeing Daddy smile. I exchanged a look with Olivia, and she nodded. Since I was the one who had the package in my hand, I was the one who was going to do the honours.

"Daddy, we got something for you," I said.

"What would that be, Princess?" he asked, and I removed it from the little bag I was holding.

"Open it," I encouraged with a smile. Daddy looked at weirdly because it was a ring box. I'm pretty sure he had completely misunderstood. I fought the urge to laugh. Daddy opened the gift, and the expression on his face turned serious. He stared at the gift for a while then looked up at us.

"I love you too. Come here and hug me." I rushed forward and hugged him then made room for Olivia to do same.

"So, you have something to tell us? Why are you home so early?" I asked, settling myself in his lap while Olivia helped him put the necklace on.

"We are going on a trip. We are going to the Bahamas," he said, and Olivia and I looked at each other and squealed.

"Oh my God, Daddy. You're the best," she squealed, then kissed him on the mouth. I watched them as Daddy deepened the kiss, and I shifted a bit in his lap. Now was not the time to get aroused.

"When are we leaving?" I asked. I was asking all the questions because Olivia was being very, very horny, and couldn't keep her hands off Daddy.

"In about thirty minutes. So you better go pack." We stood and ran to the nursery excitedly. This was going to be fun.

***

Once again, like the first time Daddy and I went on vacation, we had use his friend's private plane. I had to admit that it was way more convenient than commercial flights. And faster. But I had never been to the Bahamas, so I didn't know about that, to be honest. The place was even more beautiful than in the pictures. Daddy had gotten us a house that had its own private beach, just like in Hawaii. It was great because that way, we were free to do whatever we wanted without people staring at us like we were weirdos.

"Go change. Let's go to the beach," Daddy said. I changed into a baby pink bikini. I hoped it would remind Daddy of the first night we were together. Then Olivia changed into a sexy one piece that had no fabric on the sides, exposing her tiny waist. We were good to go. Daddy was in swim trunks, and he looked edible. But now was not the time for such thoughts. We had to go enjoy our time on the beach.

"Kelly, you remember last time. When I call you, you listen," he said, and I nodded.

"Yes, Daddy," I said and pretended to salute him as Olivia, and I headed down towards the sea.

"What happened last time?" Olivia asked.

"Well, I almost got drowned," I explained, and she widened her eyes.

"Damn babes. Thank goodness you're okay," she said, and I hugged her. I loved this girl. We started splashing each other with water. It was fun. We kept on laughing and giggling. Then we took it up a notch. I'd splash her, then I'd touch her crotch a little a giggle. She'd do same to me and rub my nipple. We kept on doing that until Daddy called. We turned and looked, but he was coming our way.

"Why don't you include me in that?" James asked. Olivia and I smiled, and each of us started splashing him with water, without giving him the chance to get a hold of us. We were having so much fun, then he caught me.

"I've caught you now," he said creepily, and I shrieked.

"Daddy!!" We laughed and then all of a sudden, he kissed me. He opens his mouth slightly, inviting me to deepen the kiss. He tastes like the island around us; the tang of brine and the sweetness of fruit. Warmth radiates from his body, enveloping me, protecting me. I circle my hands up his neck, tangling them in the long locks of soft hair. He pulls his lips away from my own, breaking the kiss. My eyes snap open in protest but close in pleasure once again when he begins trailing kisses along my jawbone, pausing to suckle at the soft corners of my ear. I trace the curve of his spine, reveling in the coils of muscle beneath my fingertips. I stop when I reach his hips, which are so agonizingly close to my own. I reach beneath him to untie the drawstring on his shorts, but quick hands stop me.

"Not yet," he whispers in my ear, warm breath tickling the wisps of hair around it. He grabs my wrists, one in each hand, and brings them up above my head. I stare at him in confusion, but my inquiring gaze is only met with a mischievous grin. He trails his hands lightly down my arms, fingertips just barely making contact, down to my waist, before circling back up to the curve of my breasts. He traces them lightly over my bikini, the brief contact sending my nipples to attention. Deft hands untie the knots behind my back and around my neck, allowing him to pull away the thin material in a single sweeping motion. The cool air on my naked breasts releases a sigh of contentment from me; I have never had them exposed outside. He cups my right breast in one hand, massaging the nipple with his thumb, while his tongue teases my left; he flicks and circles it with his tongue, and I moan, unable to repress the pang of pleasure the motion is sending down my navel. I hook one leg around his waist, raising my hip to meet him. A low moan grumbles in his throat, and he firmly pushes me down again; he lifts his eyes to mine as he slides down my body, kissing my belly, moving lower and lower.

"I said not yet," he whispers, pulling away my bikini bottoms with nimble fingers. At this point, Olivia straddles my face and lowers her dripping wetness unto my mouth. I start lapping it up, making sure to nip at her clit a little. Daddy buries his face between my thighs, sucking, and licking, skilfully flicking his tongue over my pearl. I arch my back in ecstasy, moaning as waves of pleasure roll over my body. I grasp my breast with one hand, digging into the flesh, while the other runs through his hair. He's moaning, and It's almost enough to send me over the edge. With Olivia still riding my face, Daddy guides himself into me, slowly at first, the tip of his cock just barely teasing my entrance, before filling my core with a rough groan of relief that tells me he wants this as much as I do. He rocks his hips into mine, gently, and steadily. Then faster, and harder, his breath mingling with mine, gasping, moaning, a mixture of pain and pleasure. Our arms and legs are entwined.

I moan into Olivia's wetness, holding her legs up as Daddy continues pounding me with an urgency that reverberates through my bones. The heat between my thighs builds and builds until I can't take it any longer; my body tenses and shudders, a shiver running down my spine as my body collapses into a pool of gratification. He muscles tensed tightly, not long after, groaning loudly as he spills his cum deep within me. We, me, him, Olivia, crumble together in the sand, still entwined, slick with sweat. Faces close together. I can feel him smiling behind my closed eyes, a tightening of his grasp on me as his breath falls into the steady rhythm of sleep. The crash of waves on the shoreline is the last thing I hear before joining him in slumber.

When I woke up I was back in the beautiful hotel room lying on the king-size bed in the middle of the bedroom. James had really outdone himself with this vacation. I could hear Olivia playing in the living room and James on the balcony talking on the phone. I stayed in bed, listening to the waves crash on the shore and sighed in contented bliss.

"Daddy," I called as I yawned and stretched after hearing him end his phone call. Suddenly, I was greeted by the sight of James, only wearing a towel around his hips. He ran his fingers through his hair and smiled at me.

"Hey baby girl. You had a big sleep. Ready to have a bath and then join Oli playing in the living room. She has been building a big tower that I'm sure she will let you help make," James said as he came over to me and picked me up in his arms. I loved how strong he was and snuggled into him as he carried me to the bathroom.

Placing me down in the bath, he ran warm water over my sleepy body and washed me clean before drying me off with one of the fluffy white hotel towels and wrapping me in one of the bathrobes.

"Such a pretty girl," James said as he led me back to the bedroom. He placed me on the floor and opened my bathrobe. Sliding a diaper under my hips as I quietly obeyed his gentle taps to move me this way and that. I liked that he knew that it took me a while before I was able to come out of my sleepy state. He powdered me and fastened the diaper around my waist before placing me in one of the onesies he had packed for me. It was pink with clouds on it, and I loved how he always knew which one I wanted to wear.

After he had finished dressing me, he put my paci in my mouth and watched as I made a beeline for the living room. I had not forgotten that James had said Olivia was building a block tower, and I was very interested in being part of that process.

I crawled along the carpeted floor to the living room and sat next to Olivia. She threw her arms around me and held me tight, pulling me into her lap and continuing to play. Her little age was older than mine, and she liked being a bigger than me. I didn't mind, it was nice to be the baby. Everything was perfect, and life was only just getting started.

Who is Tina Moore?

Tina Moore has enjoyed the lifestyle of a Mommy Domme for several years. She began exploring kink and BDSM in her youth and found her love of being a strict Mommy Domme in early 2000. Tina Moore is now an author of many MDLG, DDLG and ABDL themed novels.

Follow her on:

Author Page on Amazon

Instagram @tinamoore.kdp

If you enjoyed this book, it would be much appreciated if you leave **a review on Amazon**.

CPSIA information can be obtained
at www.ICGtesting.com
Printed in the USA
LVHW021051041119
636249LV00002B/398